COMFORT ZONE

A Tale of Suspense

Stephen Bentley

Hendry Publishing

Bacolod City, Philippines

Dedicated to Zabrina, my wife.

"Mental illness" is among the most stigmatized of categories.' People are ashamed of

being mentally ill. They fear disclosing their condition to their friends and

confidants-and certainly to their employers."

—ELYN R. SAKS

CONTENTS

ONE

PROLOGUE

2017

She heard the footsteps and guessed the guy was about ten yards behind her. *It must be a man. They are too heavy for a woman.* Another few hundred yards and she would reach safety – her garden flat home. *I swear, no more drug runs for Ben Turner*, she thought. *This is too risky.* Her heart pounded faster. She could hear it thumping in her chest until the sound of her panting blocked it out. She could smell aftershave. It wasn't her cologne, nor was it her breathlessness she could now hear. Before the lights went out, she thought, *Fuck you, Ben!*

When she regained consciousness her first sensation was movement. *I'm in the boot of a car.* She was unable to see anything. *I must be blindfolded.* She tried to check for a blindfold but trying to move her arms was futile. Her hands were tied behind her back and she couldn't move her legs as they too were bound. Then she felt a searing pain in the back of her head and lost consciousness once more.

Clueless as to time, she knew she was in a strange room. It stunk of urine. In the distance she heard the low rumble of motorway traffic. Her head still hurt, her eyes unable to pierce the gloom, but she could see shadows. *The blindfold's gone.* On trying to move, she heard a scuffling noise and knew she was tied to a chair. She heard a door open but was unable to see in the dark. Then she heard footsteps walking away and heard a second door open. A few moments later, a car engine started and the headlamp beams flooded both doorways and the room with bright light, penetrating the darkness. She was forced to shield her eyes from the light by tilting her head to the side, averting her gaze. Curiosity taking over, she scrunched her eyes and made out the figure of a man in front of her. A man dressed in black, wearing a ski-mask. He held a long knife in front of him. He cut the tape across her mouth before running the blade down her cheek. She felt the blood as it ran to the corner of her mouth, giving her the metallic taste of her own blood.

"Who are you?" she asked in panic. "Is this about the drugs? Here, have them."

Removing his mask, the man in black said nothing.

With his face bathed in the light from the headlamp beam she recognised him. "Oh god, why are you doing this?" She knew then this was nothing to do with the half-kilo of cocaine in her jacket pocket belonging to Ben, her lover.

Silently, he walked a few feet to a table set against the far side of the room. Picking up the tool set on the table, he turned back to his prisoner. She screamed on seeing the chainsaw. Pulling on the cord, he fired it up, then cut off his victim's right arm at the elbow. She went into shock. Moments later the man used a blowtorch to cauterise the wound. Still, he said nothing. He cut the ties to move his unconscious captive, carrying her to a makeshift operating table in the middle of the room. Placing her on her back, he forced her mouth wide open with a clamp and using a scalpel, he cut out her tongue. Wiping his bloodied rubber gloves on his black jumpsuit, he reached for a meat cleaver. With one fierce blow to her slim neck, he cut right through skin, muscle, sinew and bone. Her head now rolling on the table, he was satisfied she was dead. Still he said nothing.

Bloody murder over, he left the room. His car was parked outside the deserted outbuilding, one of the few remnants of an abandoned former airfield close to a motorway twenty miles away from London. He opened the boot of his car, pulled out a black plastic refuse sack and removed his jumpsuit and gloves, placing them inside the sack. Any casual observer would have also seen two other clean jumpsuits and unused sacks.

CHAPTER 1

Within the next five days, the killer would return with two more abducted young women, the *modus operandi* identical to the first slaying except for one detail. The third victim died but was not decapitated. Her fatal wound was inflicted with the same scalpel used to cut out their tongues. He slashed the wrist of her one remaining hand after he heard a noise above the room ceiling. Checking the room above by flashlight, and satisfied the noise was caused by rats or some other vermin, he became despondent that he hadn't followed his usual method of killing.

Shrugging, he left the building for the final time, first wiping the tools clean to destroy any trace of his fingerprints. He then threw the soiled jumpsuit and bloodied gloves in the last remaining clean sack and drove home to the other side of London.

Satisfied the man in black had left, a twenty-six-year-old named Charlie Atkins dared come out of hiding. He was homeless and had been for the past ten years. He was a diagnosed schizophrenic with a history of sexual deviancy and convictions for sexual assault.

He approached the killing room slowly, reassuring himself the killer had gone. Opening the door, he flicked on his lighter to illuminate the room and saw the third victim bleeding out on the table. He was struck by her beautiful blonde hair and long legs. Pushing up her short skirt, he removed her underwear before he lay next to her on the table. He pushed her over onto her side and in a few seconds ejaculated inside her. He rolled her onto her back, so she was now gazing up with glazed lifeless eyes, ripped off her blouse and bra, then bit her breast close to her nipple. Using her underwear, he wiped himself clean. Atkins slept the rest of that night covered with old cardboard packaging in his usual spot in the room above.

Case Conference Crown Prosecution Service Harlow, Essex

"We have plenty here to charge Atkins with the three murders. What else do you want? There's his sperm inside the anus of the last victim and his sperm on her panties. The bite mark is an identical match to him. Not to mention her blood on his clothes," Margaret Childs, Senior Crown Prosecutor said.

"I know. I know. But I'll tell you what's nagging away at me, shall I?" Detective Inspector Dick Jewell said.

"Go on."

"Why admit to having sex with a dead woman but deny killing her and the other two? Plus, I don't believe he's capable of dreaming up this story about the mystery man in black who he insists is the true killer," the inspector said. "And tell me how he got all three to the abandoned airfield. He has no car and can't even drive. We know all three women ... all respectable professionals ... must have been abducted in London, then taken to the airfield. Then there's the cocaine. Half a kilo on the first victim and small amounts in the pockets of the other two. How is all this connected to drug trafficking? I don't get it. We are missing something."

"That's for his legal team to ponder, not us. We have ample evidence to charge him and there's a realistic prospect of conviction," Childs said.

"I suppose so, but these murders have all the hallmarks of ritualistic killings."

"No suppose about it, and what about Atkins' fingerprints all over the weapons: the chainsaw, scalpel, and cleaver? And the blowtorch, let's not forget that," the lawyer pointed out.

"Okay, you're right. I have checked all the databases for similar killings anywhere in Europe and drawn a blank. I guess we have no choice but to go with what we have," DI Jewell said.

"Correct! Anyway, it's a racing certainty Atkins will end up locked away in Broadmoor subject to a hospital restriction order. He's a danger to the public and a known schizophrenic."

THREE

CHAPTER 2

2019

Hunching down into my favourite navy-blue, woollen overcoat didn't help. I could still feel the biting easterly cut right through me. The bright sunshine was deceptive. I shuddered, thinking of the warm home I had left behind. The trouble was I had no idea how much longer I could call it home. Not that it seemed like much of a home since my wife died, but at least she insisted I got that old gas central heating boiler replaced with a new one. Just a shame Liz is not around to enjoy the warmth. Walking past the market's food stalls, I could smell the roast pork sandwiches. The smell reminded me of the Sunday lunches we once enjoyed at home. I was alone with my thoughts on a bitterly cold November day... in Hounslow of all places. There was a fuzzy noise in my head. I found it difficult to concentrate.

"White noise, I guess. That's what it is," I said aloud, causing an old lady to stare at me as if I was crazy.

Perhaps I am. Revenge... and murder are in my heart, mind, body and soul, and I don't totally understand why. I sense a part of me is missing, and it isn't the obvious – Liz, the only woman I ever loved aside from my mother, of course.

I have no clue as to what is happening. I can feel it, but can't see it, nor can I identify it. It is there, though. There is SOMETHING splitting me in two. It's a tug o' war. Like good on one side. Evil on the opposite side. Good to the left of me, evil to the right... I silently hummed, in tune with the Stealers Wheel song.

The noise invaded my head, rendering logical thinking impossible. Looking down at my feet I walked on, the rest of me following in robotic movements. I was on autopilot. Roaming around the open market I must have looked like a zombie with sunglasses.

Fourteen years of practice at London's Criminal Bar had taught me west London's Hounslow Heath Car Boot market was a den of iniquity. Most things, legal and illegal, could be found here – at a price. Stolen goods, drugs, guns, pirated DVDs, sex workers, contract killers and what I was searching for – a bomb maker. You just had to know where to look or who to ask without ending up in hospital, or worse.

My mind cleared for a while. I could hear the market sounds merging into one cacophony of Babel-like tongues rising then falling like a furious sea lashing a rocky shore. I was faintly aware of the immigrants' yells and calls as they crashed through my mind's white noise. The market was a magnet for London's immigrants, old and new, Somalis and east Europeans counting as the new with Jamaicans, Pakistanis and Bangladeshis the old. The eastern Europeans were of interest to me. I had an inkling I needed a Russian. Not any Russian, but preferably a former Spetsnaz or GRU agent. I say an 'inkling' because I knew I was going to kill and I knew who, but I didn't know why, how, when or where. I didn't wish to harm anyone but... it was the voice in my head. I had to.

A voice startled me. "Mister Mercer, what brings you here?" It snapped me out of the fugue on hearing my name spoken in a Cockney dialect.

"Just looking, Dave." I recognized Dave Walton as one of my old clients I had defended at the Old Bailey some years back. It seemed like he was now selling smuggled cigarettes at the market, judging by the cartons on his stall table.

"I know this place like the back of me hand. So, fart and give me a clue and I might be able to point yer in the right direction."

I chuckled at the colourful language and decided to seek help. "Russians. Do you know any or where they hang out?"

"Russian girls?"

"No, nothing like that. Just Russians."

"Gotcha. You need an interpreter."

I nodded. *How do I explain the inexplicable?*

"Try over there. The stall selling the golf clubs. Don't buy the snide though. They do 'ave some genuine but obviously they're half-inched."

I did a quick take on the rhyming slang of "half-inched" meaning pinched as in stolen before smiling. "Thanks, Dave. Golf clubs in winter?"

"Yeah. Crazy eh? Lots of golf nuts like to go to places like Portugal and Spain in winter, though."

"Suppose... how's the wife these days?"

"Fucked off. Good riddance, but thanks for asking, Mister Mercer."

"Sorry to hear that."

"I'm not," Dave laughed. "Take care now, Mister Mercer. Those Russians are heavy. Don't fuck with them. Wouldn't want you to get killed or nuthin'. You're okay, not like those posh boy barristers."

"Thanks, Dave. I'll take your advice. Dave, one other thing."

"What's that, Mister Mercer?"

"I hope you're staying away from railway tracks these days."

"Haha! You remember."

"How could I forget? You were banged up for a burglary to feed your habit. You told me how desperate you were to get clean as you tried to do away with yourself. I could not help pissing myself when you told me how you lay down on the tracks waiting for the next train to come along. That's when you delivered the punch line, 'Trouble was, Mister Mercer,' you said, 'the railway porter looked down at me from the platform. He shrugged and said, 'Mate, you've missed the last train.'"

We both laughed at the memory before Dave spoke again. "You're all right, you know. As I said, better than those posh boys. They know fuck all about real people."

Reminding myself it was partly the "posh boy barristers" that brought me to the market cleared my head. I started for the stall pointed out by Dave, but not before I turned around to speak to him once more as I recalled my erstwhile client was one of the most agile burglars in London. That triggered something, an idea, in my mind.

"Dave, are you clean these days?"

"Been clean for years, governor."

"Good. I may have something for you if you are interested. It'll pay well."

"Dodgy?"

"Yes. Give me your mobile number."

Dave scribbled it down, thrusting the scrap of paper in my outstretched palm.

FOUR

CHAPTER 3

Arriving at the stall, I saw rows of golf clubs in branded bags set out on display on a stepped table. A young woman who seemed to be a sales assistant smiled. Encouraged, I removed my gloves and took one club out of a bag, then I felt a hand grasp my shoulder.

"You look? Timewaster or buy?" The voice was deeply accented and sounded Russian, but I was no linguistics expert. Turning to the voice, I was surprised to see a slight, even wiry man about five feet ten inches tall with shoulder length hair. I had been expecting a larger, heavier, and shaven headed man to accompany the voice.

"I don't know yet. I'd like to have a proper look." I felt emasculated by this weak response. Looking around, I noticed the smiling young woman had gone. Drawing a deep breath, I added, "Look. Is there somewhere private we can talk? I have a business offer you may be interested in."

The Russian did not answer. He turned towards a large, white VW Transporter van at the back of the stall and whistled loudly. A larger, heavier, and shaven headed man hopped out of the van's passenger door. He walked to me, grunting something in Russian. Sticking a gun into my back or what I thought was a gun, he prodded and pushed me inside the back of the van.

Pushing me on to an old torn armchair, the two Russians jumped into the back and locked the door from the inside. I watched the two have a heated debate in their native language. I found that weird. Not them speaking in Russian; it was, and only for a split-second, as if I could understand every word.

I sat silent until the shaven-headed Russian spoke to me in clear but heavily accented English. "Who are you? What do you want?"

"I'm not Trading Standards looking for counterfeit goods, nor am I a cop." That was true, but I didn't volunteer the fact I was Intelligence Corps and worked undercover in the army before becoming a barrister.

"I didn't ask you who you aren't. I asked who you are."

"I'm a barrister. I defend people accused of crimes."

"I know what a barrister is. What brings you here?"

"I need help."

"What kind of help?"

"I need to know how to make bombs."

"You can do that by using Google."

"Yes, but I need to know from an expert about different types of explosions."

"You want to kill people by bomb?"

"No. I want to destroy buildings."

"Not kill people?"

"Yes, but not by bomb."

"Are you crazy?"

"Probably."

I probably am. I had no idea I wanted to destroy buildings rather than kill people by bombs until now. It was a voice somewhere inside me telling me to say that. Not a voice, THE voice.

The Russians, looking at each other, shrugged, before my interrogator said, "You wait here."

The bald Russian returned after five minutes. "Sergei," he said to his compatriot, "go check the stall. Make sure that girl doing her job." Now I was left alone with one Russian.

"Dave, the cigarette guy, vouched for you. Lucky for you."

"I'm not a spy or a cop or anything else. I am who I say I am. I only need expert help. Nothing more."

"What about materials?"

"Materials?" I echoed. *What does he mean?*

"How you going to blow something up without materials, explosives, detonators?"

I now felt stupid but also relieved. The Russian was taking all this seriously. "Yes, of course. How stupid of me."

There followed a long silence, discomforting me. The bald Russian scratched his chin, deep in thought.

"Five thousand plus materials," the Russian said eventually.

"Okay."

"No, not okay yet. We meet next week. You tell me more. I can then instruct you and I will know what you need."

"Materials, you mean?"

"Yes."

"Meet where?"

"I will get message to you."

"How?"

"Leave that to me."

"Okay."

"One other thing, Philip Mercer, you mess around with us and you will die a horrible death."

I just knew the Russian was talking about death by nerve agent. I shuddered inside.

FIVE

CHAPTER 4

The Russian was only the first stage of my plan. *What plan? You didn't have one until you met the Russians. Am I crazy?* A thought I had many times lately. I think even my wife was worried about me before she fell ill. She kept asking if I felt all right, telling me I had started muttering and shouting in my sleep. I don't remember any dreams, but perhaps she was right to worry as I did occasionally wake with what I would call night terror sweats.

I truly didn't care anymore. They were going to pay. The *they* were people who had slighted me. Cheated me. Not supported me. After fourteen years at London's Criminal Bar, I was facing ruin through bankruptcy.

Bankruptcy *per se* wasn't the problem. It was possible to continue at the Bar after bankruptcy.

The real problem was that damn interview with the Insolvency Service. I knew I had omitted financial information at that interview with the Official Receiver. An omission to protect my Liz owing to her slowly dying with cancer. It didn't matter the omission happened at the instigation of the interviewing officer. None of it was recorded, unlike a suspect's interview in a police station. There was no way of proving I had adopted the officer's words after I told him I did not have that requested information but would later supply it. Instead, the officer, wanting to draw the interview to a close in a 'tick-box' exercise, suggested I use the phrase "and other expenses" when accounting for the disposal of money from the sale of the matrimonial home some eight years before the date of the interview. That phrase will come to ruin my career and reputation if I do nothing.

In my mind, I formed a list of all the people who would pay. That part was easy. The sleepless nights weren't caused by who but striving to formulate a plan of execution to exact revenge. *How to execute the execution?*

That was the difficult part. I smiled at the wordplay. *Am I crazy?*

CHAPTER 5

Claire Munro and Deidre Summers were the first names on the list. I graduated from law school with them. Both are solicitors now. Solicitors 'brief' barristers in that they send case papers and instructions for a named barrister to represent the client in court. It doesn't require advanced skills to recognise how important they are to barristers. We formed part of a friendly cabal at law school and socialised as a group. Naturally, I thought I could rely on Munro, less on Summers, as a source of regular work and income. Munro specialised in crime in a north London firm of solicitors. Summers joined a central London firm specialising in civil litigation.

In my early days at the Bar, Munro did brief me... once. I successfully defended an old lag with a brilliant defence when the client should truly have been convicted. In vain, I expected more work from Munro. Apart from one further resoundingly successful case some years later, it never happened. Munro set up her own firm and became successful beyond her wildest dreams. The success was not the result of her intellectual ability as that was severely diminished. Instead, it was due to her attractive looks and flirtatious manner which led to detectives recommending felons to go to her firm to gain her attention and a backhander for the introduction. She soon forgot her old friends like me.

Munro also practised the dark arts of getting clients to switch representation. Promises were made to youths in custody awaiting trial, a new pair of the latest 'must have' running shoes the prize for changing the approved legal firm to hers. The shoes would be delivered to the prison by friend or family. The recipient was delighted, and her firm gained a new client. She also had a dodgy boyfriend. I mean, *really* dodgy. He was a drug dealer moving serious amounts of cocaine, heroin and amphetamines all over north London. She idolised him and went to any lengths to help and protect him. I think his name is Ben.

Summers was in a different league. Early on, she did try to offer me some sops, but I was neither impressed nor pacified. They were piffling small claims cases in the county court, far removed from crime and defending in front of judge and jury. Over several drinks one night I berated her about this. She was starting to make a name for herself in libel cases. I pointed out to her these cases were adjudicated by juries, so the skills of a criminal barrister were just as valid in that arena as they were in a criminal trial. I mentioned the successes of George Carman QC to bolster my argument.

Summers scoffed at all this and never sent me any more briefs. Come to think of it, I had much in common with Carman. We were both down to earth Lancastrians, fond of booze, and preferred the company of women over men. Summers and Munro surely knew all this. She was also the only person who mentioned my lopsided jaw. It got broken playing rugby, ending up with me speaking out of the side of my mouth, but she told me I looked like a male version of Drew Barrymore, implying I would not be taken seriously as an advocate. What tosh!

CHAPTER 6

I played the networking 'game' with both women, arranging tickets for prestigious sports events and never failed to invite them to any interesting 'legal get together' for new business opportunities, both theirs and mine. Eventually, I knew these efforts were futile and as my own criminal practice grew (after all, there are thousands of London solicitors), I tried hard to erase the resentment I felt towards these two women. That feeling faded with time but was never eradicated entirely. It was the voice that kept bringing up their names just like they were ghosts from my past.

Piers Allen is the stereotypical barrister. I would say he's a stuck-up snob. He's one of the posh boys who look down on the likes of anyone with a northern accent like mine. He also classifies anyone who graduated at one of the old polytechnics as an inferior beast. My *alma mater* is a university but was once a poly. It's fair to say, therefore, we could not stand each other. I never had a problem with that. The Bar of England and Wales is full of his type. What I did have a problem with was him approaching prisoners in their courtroom cells and telling them I was an undercover cop. Even if that were true, which it wasn't, it was an underhanded way of trying to undermine the relationship between the prisoner, my lay client, and the solicitor, my professional client, who often instructed Allen and me.

Piers Allen was jealous. He may have graduated from a prestigious university, but he was as thick as two short planks. This lack of intellectual capacity and insecurity caused him to bluster like the Toad character in *Flushed Away*, such a funny film. Every time I think of Piers Allen, I also think of Ian McKellen's megalomaniacal Toad: a pompous, pumped-up buffoon who walks around making wild, grandiose speeches about ruling the sewers with more than a hint of the craven idiocy of British politicians thrown in for good measure. Trouble is, McKellen was acting in an animated film, Allen is reality. Allen will no doubt end up in politics. He has the youthful good looks and the background to find a safe Tory seat in the shires. The blue rinse crowd will adore him if he lives that long. He's on the list for backstabbing me.

EIGHT

CHAPTER 7

Another three barristers, two of whom are members of my chambers, as is Allen, make the list. Brad Collins, the Senior Clerk of my chambers also makes it. He supervises the other clerks and in theory, ensures as a clerking team, all briefs arriving in chambers are allocated fairly if there is no named advocate. What no one mentions is the practice of bribing the senior clerk to allocate the juiciest briefs to those barristers who contribute to Brad Collins' slush fund.

David Ramsbottom is one of the chief contributors. He's one of the senior barristers in chambers and a boring old fart to boot. At five-feet-two-inches he has that classic short man inferiority complex. I have nothing against short people. My mother was five-feet-nothing. Ramsbottom is insufferable in his ways. He constantly grooms his silly little moustache and silver coiffure. He also finds it impossible to walk past a mirror without casting admiring glances at his reflection. He's another who likes the ladies and one in particular.

She is Lucy Fairweather, a barrister with long, shapely legs, and a mane of golden hair. Male solicitors instruct her because of her looks and in the hope they may get their leg over. I dare say some have succeeded. Lucy may please the eye but she's too aggressive in her courtroom style. She's like a car with only one gear, unable to select more appropriate ways to tackle a problem. I have defended with her a few times. On occasions, I half expect her to challenge a prosecution witness as to the veracity of the witness's name: *"Are you sure you are John Smith?"* she snarls, stabbing an accusatory finger towards the hapless witness. I believe her aggression partly stems from her use of cocaine.

Brad Collins had me down as junior barrister to be led by Ramsbottom in a multi-handed murder trial. It would have paid handsomely. I say 'would' because it never happened because of Ramsbottom's intervention. He asked Collins, the senior clerk, to switch Lucy as his junior rather than me. The trial was scheduled for eight weeks in Lancashire involving all trial counsel, at least those from London, staying at a Manchester hotel for the duration. Ramsbottom wanted to increase the chances of getting his leg over.

Finbar Keogh is another barrister on my list. He stole a lucrative murder brief from me, but more of that later. *The voice* is telling me to add Jeffrey to the list. At first, I hadn't got a clue who he was, but *the voice* remonstrated with me: The Official Receiver guy. The one who conned you at the bankruptcy interview.

He should be first on the list. I know that, but how the hell do I contact him, never mind get close enough to kill him?

NINE

CHAPTER 8

Taking the Tube's Piccadilly Line from Hounslow West, I got off at Green Park, changing to the Victoria Line for Brixton. Walking up Brixton Hill, I stopped at the takeaway curry house as I remembered it was a Sunday, my helper's day off. Kasia cleaned my home as well as cooking sometimes. I often cook myself, having learned from my mother and brother who were excellent cooks. Slow cooked belly pork is my speciality, a typical Sicilian *paisano* dish.

Anyway, I ordered the chicken jalfrezi, some rice and a naan bread, and a four-pack of beers to wash it down. Jimmy the owner, I think his real name is Jamal, asked me if it was still as cold outside. "Brass monkeys," I said. Truth was I couldn't wait to get home even though no one was there. Another three minutes' walk and I was letting myself in through my front door. The warm air enveloped me, reminding me of holidays in the Spanish sunshine. In turn, that filled me with sadness as it was always our plan to retire to Spain. 'Our' meaning Liz and me.

My home was built in 1910, a solid brick symbol of London suburbia. It has three bedrooms, one of which is the master with *en suite* bathroom. There is another bathroom on the landing. Downstairs is the long hall with a small WC just off the front door, a living room that was originally two rooms but made into one large room, and at the end of the hall a huge kitchen cum dining area. There is enough space for eight at the solid oak dining table. An island counter separates the cooking and eating spaces. The island contains the wine refrigerator with wine racks on the counter holding the red wine. The cooking or kitchen area is on the back wall along with a large American-style combined fridge/freezer with a water dispenser. The wall is clad in stainless-steel sheet. The utensils, also stainless-steel, hang on pegs on the sheet above the stove.

All of this was Liz's doing. She designed all of it. The new gas boiler is on the same wall but closer to the back door. That door leads out to the 'jungle', a small yard at the rear of the house, now neglected. It used to be tidy and where we barbequed but then work happened, so we didn't have the free time to BBQ. The old cut down oil drum I used to BBQ is still out there somewhere. Also, somewhere out there amongst the foliage, branches, and roots is the sewerage drain cover. I keep meaning to have it checked as there is a foul smell wafting from it when the wind blows in a certain direction. Kasia frequently mentions a peculiar smell. I forget how many times I've explained about the sewer to her. The smell is why I keep the kitchen window locked tight, as well as to foil burglars.

After hanging up my coat in the hall, I made for the kitchen, took out a plate from a drawer in the island counter and a spoon and fork to eat my curry. I popped open one of the beer cans, placing the other three into the fridge. Once I finished eating, I moved to the living room, got comfortable in my winged armchair and flicked on the TV.

The TV picture was all lines like interference. That's when I heard *the voice* once more. "Phil," he said. It was a man's voice, the same voice I had heard previously. "Phil!" it said with urgency.

"What?" I said.

"You can call me Vincent."

"Like Vincent Van Gogh?" I also thought, *How appropriate. Didn't he go mad too? Chopped off his ear, I heard.*

"Just Vincent."

"I'd prefer if you didn't talk at all."

"Oh, don't be like that. I'm helping you."

"How?"

"I'll tell you how to kill these people."

"What people?"

"C'mon, you are not stupid. The people who have ruined your life. Claire Munro, Piers Allen, Brad Collins, Lucy Fairweather, David Ramsbottom, Deidre Summers, and Finbar Keogh."

"Stop. Stop it. You're scaring me," I shouted at the TV screen. On looking up at the screen, I saw myself but different somehow. I also saw someone or something else.

"Good, you can see me now," Vincent said.

"Not good at all. I can't do any of these things. It's murder. I couldn't stand to be locked away for years."

"Phil, they deserve to die."

"They deserve to be punished, I agree, but die?"

"Yes. Look what they have put you through. Friends who haven't supported you, stole money from you."

"Stole money?"

"Yes. All those briefs that should have been yours. All of them have connived in one way or another to deprive you of what was rightfully yours. If they hadn't stolen from you, there would be no bankruptcy."

"That's true. I don't mind bombing their empty offices but killing is another matter."

"Do both. Who do you think was behind the contact with the Russians at Hounslow?"

"You?"

"Damn right, me, and Dave your old client."

Right now, I know I'm mad and want to get Vincent out of my life. I also know madness runs in my family. My grandmother was institutionalised. I'm scared. I'll tell him one thing then do the other. That might work. *Will it? I don't know, I'm so conflicted. Liz, I need you.*

"Okay, Vince. I hear you. So, what's the grand plan for me to get rid of these people once and for all?"

"Vincent, not Vince. I'll think of something. The solicitors and barristers will be easier than Jeffrey."

"Jeffrey?"

"You forgot already? The guy who conned you in the interview over your bankruptcy."

"Right, got you. Tell the truth, I'd enjoy doing him. He definitely deserves to die." I was shocked at my words, but I did mean them.

"That's the spirit. Leave it all to me. I'll be seeing you. Bye."

Vince. I prefer that to Vincent – it's less formal. The TV interference disappeared. The BBC News was on the TV in glorious colour. Zapping channels on the remote, I was unable to concentrate. There's no way I can kill these people. Like I told Vince, the thought of doing time in prison or a mental hospital is insufferable. Besides, I'm not a bad person. My whole family were good people, not bad people. I think we only have one black sheep in the family – my grandfather on my mother's side. He assaulted a copper whilst drunk many years ago. Not exactly crime of the century. I was raised with Christian values. My whole upbringing and military training were about values and standards.

I truly don't think I can do this. *Can I? Will I?*

"Fuck off, Vince!" I felt my face contort in a mixture of fear and disbelief as I mouthed the words.

CHAPTER 9

A week went by before I heard from the Russians. I was starting to hope they'd forgotten all about me. My mobile rang. No Caller ID. "Yes?" I said.

I recognised the accent immediately. "We meet next Tuesday. Do not write anything down and come alone. Three in the afternoon. The Lazy Dog in Fleet Street. The back bar." The line went dead.

I did as I was told. The back bar in question was a dark dingy hole of a place. It was one of the least popular pubs in the area. I wore my favourite navy-blue overcoat and had popped on my grey fedora before leaving home. I felt it was the sort of hat a barrister should wear. Hat or no hat, the bald Russian recognised me. He said nothing, simply held up his hand.

He was sitting at the table furthest away from the bar entrance door. Again, saying nothing, he gestured for me to sit. I sat opposite him. He stared at me, then patted a bag on the seat next to him. He whispered so softly I had a little trouble hearing him clearly. I did make out, "All here. You have money?"

"Yes."

"Give me."

"In a moment. First tell me what is in there and how I plant bombs to make buildings fall down."

"Enough C4 plastic explosive to bring down five buildings. Detonators. Ten mobile phones, all untraceable, never registered and never used. How tall are these buildings?"

"Tall?"

"Yes, how many floors, stories?"

"Two and three. One has two and the other three. Oh, the third has five."

"Okay, here's what you do. Drill holes in the · load bearing columns but close to the ceiling and how you say? RSJ - rolled steel joists... yes, RSJ. The ceiling on the lowest floor. Put the explosives inside with detonator wired to the phone. When you are ready call the phone and boom! The steel will buckle if you use enough C4 and the building will collapse under its own weight. It's called gravity."

"That sounds simple enough."

"My friend, it is not simple. You must be careful and exact. The instructions how to wire the phones to the detonators are in the bag."

"Is this stuff in the bag safe?"

"It is until you detonate it. Now, money please."

I took out the envelope containing the five-thousand cash. On handing it to the Russian, he said, "Here, open this paper and shield me." He passed me a copy of the *Times*. I didn't need instructions. I fully opened it, so the broadsheet was extended between my outstretched hands forming perfect protection from prying eyes, not that there was anyone else in the back bar.

"Okay, all here." It was only then I folded the paper and gestured to return it. "You keep," the Russian said. There was no sign of the envelope. He must have pocketed it. I waited for the 'what next,' when he spoke again. "You never see me. You make no contact with me. I know where you live,

Mercer. Just forget all about me. You wait three minutes, then you leave."

I was thinking what to say when the Russian stood and walked out of the bar and presumably out of the pub into the street. I waited five minutes before I also left, carrying a bag.

The bus home was a good idea. It gave me thinking time. I needed to come up with a plan to get them all round to my place. *Where's Vince when I need him?*

ELEVEN

CHAPTER 10

During the long bus ride home, I reflected a lot about life at the Criminal Bar of England and Wales. It brought me many pleasing memories and my fourteen-year career as a barrister was something I had worked hard at after I had left the British Army. Sure, there were many times I defended rogues and rascals, and deep down I suspected they were guilty, but that's the price you pay for the rule of law in a civilised society. Some guilty go free and, sadly, some innocents are punished. Guilty or not, they are subjected to the scrutiny of their peers. Twelve men and women selected at random to weigh the evidence in any case involving a criminal trial. Unless you can tell me of a better system, I tend to agree with the words of Lord Devlin who famously said, " ... trial by jury is more than an instrument of justice and more than one wheel of the constitution: it is the lamp that shows that freedom lives."

One of those pleasing memories didn't involve a trial. I was part heard in a long case in Leeds when I was instructed to enter a plea in mitigation for a forty-year-old woman from Zimbabwe. She had earlier pleaded guilty to a charge of forgery involving a document to show she had the necessary clearances to obtain work in England. In fact, she was an asylum seeker who had fled the Mugabe tyranny in her homeland after she saw her husband brutally butchered by Mugabe's thugs. Leaving behind her home, her two teenage daughters and all her possessions she managed to escape, travelling to Zambia, Botswana, and South Africa. During her travels she was raped, beaten and forced to work in a brothel until she escaped once more, finally getting help from a South African township criminal gang to fly to the UK on a false passport supplied by the gang.

She had wired her life savings to pay for the passport and flight to London.

Before going to see this woman in the cells before the sentencing hearing, I read the contents of the Pre-Sentence Report which covered her history. I must say I was a little sceptical until I talked to her. She turned out to be a strikingly good-looking woman, intelligent and articulate, who came from a wealthy family hence her university education in Zimbabwe. Her husband had been a vociferous political opponent of Mugabe. It was her inner calm that impressed me most. She wasn't bitter, simply desiring to be free and reunited with her two teenage daughters. That was why she sought work illegally to pay for her daughters to travel to England. She succeeded. I learned her daughters would be in court to watch the proceedings. Listening to her, I was forced to bite my lips to prevent myself from crying. It was such a harrowing tale. I vowed silently to do my utmost to secure her immediate release, and on leaving the cells behind me, I dabbed my eyes with a handkerchief.

Her case was called on in front of the Recorder of Leeds, the senior judge at this Crown Court. He had a reputation as a harsh sentencer, so my heart sank when I knew it was him. The court listened as the prosecution outlined the facts of the case. Then it was my turn to mitigate on her behalf. I did so for all I was worth, unafraid to pluck a few heartstrings. I heard a few sniffles from court staff and the public gallery. The local newshounds were also scribbling furiously.

"Mister Mercer," the judge said, stopping me in mid-sentence, "do you concede that all the authorities in similar cases suggest a custodial sentence of between six to nine months?"

"I do, my Lord, but..."

"I know what you are about to say. I will follow your unspoken suggestion."

I sat down, unsure of what he was going to do but hopeful he was a good mind reader.

"Zena Moyo, stand please. You have pleaded guilty to a serious charge of forgery, forging a document to help you find work illegally. As an asylum seeker you knew you were not permitted to work in this country. However, I have read the probation report, and listened carefully to the eloquent words spoken by Mister Mercer on your behalf, but my hands are tied by sentencing precedents, therefore I sentence you to six months imprisonment.

"You have been in custody now for three months. You are automatically entitled to early release halfway through your sentence. That means you are deemed to have served your sentence and can be released immediately."

I felt like crying all over again. A quickly stifled ripple of applause was heard in the public gallery.

Checking my watch, I saw I had enough time to visit Mrs Moyo once more in the cell block before her release. Before I reached the bottom of the stairs leading to the cells, two young and beautiful women rushed for me. They hugged and kissed me. "Thank you, thank you so much," they said.

The cell block door opened to reveal Mrs Moyo walking free. "Mama, Mama," the two daughters cried. It's times like these that make me proud to know my profession can truly help people in trouble.

Often, I thought I should base my practice in the north of England. That was where my roots lay. I felt at home in the north and amongst northerners. That feeling intensified after I was instructed in a succession of cases in north of England Crown Courts. It was good to escape from London's rat race. I mooted the idea with Liz a few times. She wasn't against it but did point out that though her graphic design business was conducted from home she was often expected to meet with her mainly London-based clients. I knew that presented a difficulty and her income was a useful back up to the fluctuations in my income as a barrister. So, it was put on the back burner. I think there was another reason, too.

Liz told me we had a fight. I truly don't recall it. Liz and I fighting was a rare occurrence. She told me we argued because she was asking me what I had been doing burning stuff out in the yard. She went on to tell me I had used the old BBQ drum for burning something. I hadn't got a clue what she was talking about and it developed into a heated battle of words. She even accused me of having an affair and destroying evidence. I was gutted. It soon blew over and afterwards she seemed worried about me. I didn't understand why.

Anyway, where was I? Apart from still riding on the top deck of a London bus. Oh yes... there came a time during my frequent stints in northern courts when I started to attract groupies. One, actually. He was an elderly man who loved to while his time away watching counsel ply their trade in the courts. All the local barristers and court staff knew him. Peter was his name. He approached me outside one of the courtrooms seeking a friendly chat. I obliged him and from that moment on, I had my first and only fan. On one occasion I was surprised to see him in London – at the Royal Courts of Justice to be precise. I spoke to him, asking him what he was doing so far from his usual haunts. He said, "Mister Mercer, I've come to watch you in the Court of Criminal Appeals upstairs. I heard you had an appeal listed in front of the Lord Chief Justice. Well, I couldn't miss that." I was flattered and on returning to the north, I mentioned this to some local barristers.

"My goodness, Peter usually follows silks. You are honoured," one of them said.
These thoughts on my long bus ride, may I add, helped keep *the voice* at bay.

CHAPTER 11

The voice was now infrequent. My reminiscing about my experiences as a barrister in the north relieved the stress I had been going through. The combined stresses of bereavement and the bankruptcy. Anyway, back to reminiscing, the silks, Queen's Counsel, I met in the north were an amiable bunch except for one toffee-nosed posh boy. He was the leader of the Circuit, treated like a mini god by many. I'm not sure if that was because of his professional status or his family having owned feudal lands in North Yorkshire dating back to the Middle Ages. He gave the impression the concept of master and servant was still alive in that part of the world.

I was at one time surrounded by silks in a murder trial in the north. They included that Circuit leader. It gave me confidence in my professional competence. I was being led by a silk in a trial involving ten defendants indicted for murder. It lasted for eleven weeks. This took place in Leeds. All the defendants were running a cutthroat defence: it wasn't me who stabbed the victim to death, it was X, Y or Z. This type of defence often results in guilty verdicts for all defendants. Not only is the prosecution piling in with evidence of guilt, they are also assisted by the stance of the defendants.

My client was the subject of an application from one of his co-defendants to introduce evidence of his bad character demonstrating the real nature of cutthroat defences. Naturally, the Crown supported the application. The real difficulty was not the application itself but the new hearsay evidence laws that had recently passed into law. There were no guideline cases to guide the judge or counsel. We were in uncharted legal territory. I was being led by a London silk who should have retired years ago. At one time he was a force to reckon with, but now in his dotage he was going through the motions.

To make matters worse, he had not kept abreast with developments in the law. That was why it fell to me to make the legal arguments to prevent the jury hearing this damaging hearsay evidence. Legal argument with the jury excluded took two days to complete. I was making it all up, seeing we were all in exceptional circumstances arguing novel aspects of a new law. I was relieved when the judge made his ruling in my client's favour, but that relief turned to pride when Peter Smithson, one of the local silks, mouthed, "Well done," to me. I also noticed the snooty Circuit leader nodding his approval.

Shortly after and in the cell block interview room, the client insisted I carry on alone. He wished to sack the silk leading me. Though confident of my abilities, I persuaded the client not to insist on sacking the silk. I did that because I thought it the decent thing to do. Decency is instilled in me, partly through upbringing and partly owing to my military background. It was during this trial I encountered practices that were far removed from decent. In one example, the leading barrister for one of the defendants kept disappearing from the trial for days at a time leaving his junior in charge. It was discovered the absentee was guilty of 'double bubble,' whereby he was listed for two trials at the same time and claiming fees for both cases.

The second, and I guess there is some humour in it, involved another leading barrister who was named in a newspaper as a modern-day gigolo. He was a "pretty boy" as well as a "posh boy" barrister. He acted as a paid escort to lonely old ladies he was in the habit of picking up in expensive London hotels. His services additionally included those of the sexual kind.

I must get rid of the bag the Russian gave me, I thought.

THIRTEEN

CHAPTER 12

These fond recollections are fine, but the trial work had dried up months ago. I couldn't work after Liz died. Just couldn't face people, clients, judges, other barristers... the world. My income had almost disappeared. On returning to work after my self-imposed exile, I was given scraps by my clerks in chambers. A Pleas and Directions Hearing there or a Mention here. None of those court appearances were my own work. I was standing in for assigned trial counsel who, for one reason or another, was unavailable on these hearing days. They paid a pittance. In fact, I lost money with some after deducting travel expenses to some far-flung court in the provinces.

My working day, therefore, often finished at midday or earlier. If the court hearing was in London, I was home by one in the afternoon at the latest. Gone were the days when it was my practice, like all other normally-functioning barristers, to call in at my chambers to check for new briefs, correspondence, to find out what was in my diary for the following days or weeks and perhaps even to socialise both in chambers or over a few beers at a local hostelry. It was depressing.

One full week had gone by since I met the Russian. I had hidden the bag in the attic at home. It was now getting close to Christmas, oh what joy! The thought of a Christmas alone at home made me want to puke. The anticyclone that had brought the near-Siberian conditions to Britain was still hovering. It was motionless, sitting off the west coast of Ireland. Every day was the same – bitterly cold with bright blue skies. Boy was I grateful for the central heating on walking through my front door. It was the only thing that cheered me up even if it was a fleeting feeling. The warmth was in stark contrast to the coldness I felt deep inside me.

I wasn't always like that. I used to enjoy life to the full; married life, family occasions, and most of all working with people in the military I trusted with my life. The smile had been removed from my soul. Three deaths and bankruptcy tend to have that effect. Not just any old deaths, mind you. The three most important people in my life – my wife, mother and brother, all gone in the space of two years.

Flopping in the armchair at home I reflected on these things while half-listening to some inane chat show on the TV. That was when Vince appeared again. First, I heard him, then the same fuzzy TV interference enabled me to see his face in the set. It was like looking in the mirror, but Vince seemed older than me. He also looked angry.

"I have it," he said.

"Have what?"

"How to get them all together."

"Go on," I said, irritated.

"A dinner party, here. At your home."

"And?"

"You kill them."

"How?"

"That's up to you."

"Why a dinner party?"

"You are all friends or were at one time. You're a dab hand in the kitchen. Why wouldn't they want to come? Arrange it for late January. Get Christmas out of the way first. People love an excuse to go out at that time because the full-on Christmas and New Year festivities seem like distant memories."

"Hmm. Yes, it could work."

"I also have another idea. An after-dinner parlour game."

"Like charades?"

"No. A storytelling game."

"What?"

"Get them to be frank and tell the whole room what truly scares them."

"I get it. I already know what scares the two solicitors. We played a similar game at university."

"There you go! But that was for fun. This time it gives you the opportunity to kill them all."

"Can't I just blow up the offices where they work?"

"There's no retribution in that, for goodness sakes. Only inconvenience. Their lives will eventually get back to normal and you will still be hating them for all they have done to you."

"Vince?"

"My name is Vincent, not Vince."

"Right, Vincent. Why me?"

"You need help. You're not well, not yourself. Do you want help or not?"

"Yes, I do. I can't think straight. My world is spinning. Some days I feel like screaming… or worse."

Vince, as I prefer to call him, disappeared as swiftly as he had arrived. If he hadn't been real and truly talking to me, I'd think I was crazy. But I still baulked at the plan to kill those people until I opened the letter.

CHAPTER 13

On returning home, it was lying on the carpet inside the front door along with some bills. I picked all the mail up, absent-mindedly placing the pile on a coffee table next to my armchair in the living room. I singled it out to open first as it didn't seem to be a bill. Flipping it over, I read 'Department of Business and Innovation' on the back of the envelope. Funny how government departments change names through time. It used to be the 'Department of Trade and Industry,' but now Britain has next to no industry to mention, some innovator changed the name. What I read next was far from amusing. It was a summons for me to appear at court on the third of February next to answer a charge of perjury. My worst fear had come true. The Official Receiver interview and the one answer I gave was the basis for the charge of perjury. This not only meant the end of my career as a barrister, but moreover the real prospect of time behind bars.

I felt sick to my stomach. The white noise returned inside my head for a few minutes before clearing. All was now clear – Vince was right. I will kill them all and blow up their offices for good measure.

Picking up my mobile, I dialled Dave's number. He answered.

"Dave, it's me. Phil. Phil Mercer."

Dave agreed to come to my home. I needed privacy to formulate the bomb plot with him. Besides, I didn't wish to carry the bag through London again.

Dave arrived at seven that evening. I sat him down in the kitchen but not before offering him a beer. "I'd love one, Mister Mercer."

Walking over to the fridge, I corrected him, "Just Phil, okay?"

"Fine. Old habits die hard."

Pulling the tabs off both cans of beer, I placed one in front of him before I sat opposite at the dining table.

"Remember I told you I might have something for you the day I bumped into you at Hounslow market?"

"Of course."

"What would you say if I asked you to blow up three buildings?"

"Four things. Are you nuts? Which buildings? Does anyone get hurt? How much?"

"Three of those are easy to answer. Maybe I am nuts. I don't know. No one gets hurt. Twenty-thousand."

"Cash?"

"Up front."

"Tell me more."

"Before I do, I need to fetch a bag from the attic."

"Mister... I mean Phil. I'm not going anywhere."

As I placed the bag on the table, Dave said, "What's in that?"

"Wait up, and I'll tell you."

I unzipped the bag, slowly removing the contents – the packages of C4 explosive, detonators, mobile phones, and instructions.

Dave emitted a low whistle. "Fuck me. There's enough to blow up the Houses of Parliament. You ain't a commie, is ya?"

"No. I'm not Catholic either."

"Eh?"

"Guy Fawkes was a Catholic."

"Gotcha."

"The thing is, Dave, I need to know you can do this. I know you are or were one of the best burglars in south London, but can you plant the explosives?"

"I can do it. What about detonating? Is that what the phones are for?"

"Exactly. You drill a hole, pack in the explosive, fix the detonator wired to one of the phones. You can be anywhere you want to be when you call that phone. I suggest the further away the better before it goes boom!"

"These instructions? They tell me how to wire the detonator?"

"Yes."

"What about ten grand a building? Thirty total?"

I did some quick maths in my head, thinking about what was in my savings account. "It's a deal. Just one thing, though."

"Yes?"

"You buy the drill."

Over the next hour or so, I talked Dave through the best place to fix the explosives to ensure the upper floors collapsed in on the building. He knew what I was talking about, having spent some years in the construction industry. More to the point, I was convinced he was the right choice when he added enthusiastically, "Not sure what they say about RSJs in these notes. Better in one of the load-bearing columns. Whether they are concrete, brick or stone, they will bend with the explosion. In that way, they lose their load bearing ability and crash, bang, wallop. The building's flat as a pancake."

"You're in charge, Dave. It has to be done on one specific evening – January twenty-fifth."

"When do I get the thirty grand?"

"Take the bag and all this stuff with you. Hide it well. I'll call you and arrange for you to collect the cash from me here, okay?"

"Sounds good to me. What's in it for you?"

"Let's just say I have some old scores to settle. I'll also give you the keys to my chambers in Holborn. That will mean one less building to break into. You've been there before for a conference with me, remember?"

"Yeah. Where's the other two?"

"Wait," I said as I went to the hall to pick up the Yellow Pages. Returning to the dining room table. I scribbled down two addresses after checking in the directory. One was Claire Munro's solicitor firm's office and the other the Insolvency Office building.

Taking in the details, Dave said, "Okay. Two in Holborn and one in Islington. Good. They are close to each other. Just as well. I don't wanna invoice you for travel expenses." That's one thing above all else I always liked about Dave – he had a sense of humour. As much as I wanted to laugh, I couldn't. This had turned serious. The point of no return.

FIFTEEN

CHAPTER 14

The next day there were snow flurries. I set off early for another humdrum court hearing. It was at Woolwich Crown Court in southwest London, one of the few London courts I drove to as it was a bit of a pain travelling there on the train. It was okay getting as far as the station at Woolwich Arsenal but from there it was a poor bus service.

Parking my car first, and after doing my thing in the barristers' robing room donning the horsehair wig, gown, and changing my shirt collar for the white, starched winged collar with accompanying equally starched white bands, I made my way to the cafeteria for a coffee and some toast. First, I checked the court list for my case. I was listed before His Honour Judge Charles. That brought bad memories flooding back. I suppressed them. Instead, I read the sports pages over my toast and coffee. The words went in but were jumbled, like with a dyslexic.

Thirty minutes later, I was standing in Judge Charles's court addressing him on trial dates. Not my brief, so I had a diary for trial counsel to attempt to accommodate the trial so instructed counsel may attend. The hearing lasted ten minutes. On leaving the courtroom, one of the ushers handed me a note. It was from the judge, requesting I come and see him in his chambers during the mid-morning break. I whispered to the usher, "Tell him I will be there."

The courtroom was now empty save for the clerk of the court and the note-bearing usher. On seeing me, she said, "Follow me, Mister Mercer."

As she knocked on a door in a corridor at the rear of the courtroom, I heard the stentorian tone of, "Come in." *Same old Charles*, I thought. *Captain of the ship.*

Removing my wig as custom dictated, I entered his private room. "Sit down," Judge Charles commanded like the Royal Navy officer he once was. I hadn't quite made the chair when he asked, "Mercer, how are you?"

"I'm okay, Judge."

"Sure? You don't look too ship-shape."

"Really, I'm okay. I must admit I'll be better when my practice gets back to what it once was."

"That's why I asked to see you. I vividly recall the last time you were here in my chambers. You had just got the news your brother had died. That must have been two years ago."

"Yes, it was, and I did take your advice to inform my mother in person rather than tell her over the phone. That wasn't a pleasant experience."

I chose not to elaborate. What was the point? There was nothing this judge could do to change anything. My thoughts went back in time. A time filled with painful memories.

Taking the call on my mobile phone, I was surprised to hear her voice. It was my sister-in-law calling from Australia. I steadied myself mentally as I knew there was some bad news about to be conveyed. It was shocking news. It shook me to the core. Barry, the younger brother I loved, had suddenly collapsed and died on an Australian golf course. He had married and emigrated to Australia in his twenties. Though we were separated by thousands of miles, we spoke to each other by telephone weekly. We were close. On hearing the news, the whole world moved into slow-motion. Before the call was terminated, Petra, Barry's wife said, "Will you let Mum know?" She meant my mother.

"Yes, of course." I was filled with dread.

I recall clearly that was the point when I knew I had to see Judge Charles in private. I had started a trial in his court where I was prosecuting rather than defending. I occasionally took on prosecution work if the Crown Prosecution Service saw fit to instruct me. After all, barristers were hired guns and I was no exception. In the privacy of his chambers, the judge advised me to inform my mother in person. He added that because no jury was yet sworn-in, it was fine to find a substitute barrister to prosecute the case if my professional client, the CPS agreed. On entering the CPS office, I gave no one the opportunity to disagree. To me, it was inconceivable there was any alternative to me driving to my mother's home that day and delivering the bad news. The substitute barrister was found. I assured him it was a simple case of assault and he would be up to speed by lunch time, adding I was sure Judge Charles would allow him that time to prepare. I was right.

The drive to Hampshire from Woolwich Crown Court was on autopilot. On ringing the doorbell at Mum's home, she looked surprised to see me. Then the surprise turned to fear, a look of trepidation. I think she knew what was coming. We walked through into Mum's living room. She sat in her favourite armchair. It used to be Dad's but since he died, Mum commandeered it. It was probably a comforter as well as comfortable.

"There's no other way to tell you this, Mum." Her expression turned to blank. "Barry," her eyes widened on hearing his name, "he's dead, Mum."

She did not or could not speak. The howl wasn't human. It was the noise of a mother's heart torn asunder. The noise started somewhere in the depths of her soul, forcing its anguished scream upwards until its release into the world. It shook me and there was nothing I could do. Her broken heart proved fatal. Twelve months to the day later, Mum died.

Now, I was back in the judge's private room. I said nothing about my mother to Judge Charles. I was startled by the court usher's voice, "Coffee, Judge, and for Mister Mercer. Your favourite biscuits today too."

First thanking the usher, he turned to me. "You were military police, I believe. A snowdrop or redcap?"

"Redcap for two years, then army Intelligence Corps."

"Served in Afghanistan?"

The white noise hit me. It took over. My mind was vaguely blank except there was something... something at the back of my mind. I felt it... the fear, and an overwhelming sense of wanting to please – to comply.

"What do you mean, Vincent?" the judge said. I could see a frown and a furrowed brow had replaced his usual friendly features.

"Judge, I have no idea what you are saying... Vincent?"

"That's what you just said... well, shouted rather than spoke. No matter. I asked if you had served in Afghanistan."

"No, never did, sir."

"Sir? Are you all right, Mister Mercer?"

"My wife died too. Did you know that?"

I didn't wait for an answer. I spoke as if it was an empty room. God knows what the judge was thinking.

"Yes, three deaths in two years." I could hear my voice, but it was disembodied, a bit like hearing a faint echo. I think I gave him the abridged version of the story. I believe this is what I said.

Liz and I married while we were both in the Army. She was also in the Corps but on the training side. She made Captain and I was a Sergeant. That's how we met but funny thing, I don't recall our first date. We never had kids you know. After leaving the Army, I went to law school and was called to the Bar. She worked from home as a graphic designer. At first, we could only afford a flat in Kingston Upon Thames, but my practice took off and her freelancing gig also started to flourish so we moved to the house in Brixton. Things were great but then she was diagnosed with breast cancer.

That was just before my brother died. No biggie, we thought, breast cancer can be treated. Well, it was. Radiotherapy, chemo, surgery – the lot. I guess she was one of the unlucky ones. It had spread and continued spreading until it ate her up. Before she died, she weighed five stone nothing. It broke my heart to see her suffering like that. To make matters worse, and after I had ignored statutory demands for unpaid income tax and late return penalties, I was declared bankrupt. Now, pray tell if you know anyone who can concentrate on tax when his wife is lying next to him slowly dying. It got worse. I attended the Insolvency

Service interview in their Holborn office after the bankruptcy. During the interview, not tape-recorded, I was asked about proceeds from the sale of the flat. I knew they had been used to buy our Brixton home, but I was asked for exact amounts. I couldn't recall. That's when the guy interviewing me feigned the 'good old friendly chap' routine. He told me to say the proceeds went on "and other expenses." I wasn't too comfortable with that, but he point-blank assured me I could rectify the information at any future time. That was my plan. To get out of there reserving my position to safeguard Liz from any further shocks of a financial nature in the full knowledge I could add the required details at some future point. Liz died in my arms before that point arose.

Then I was conscious of saying, "It backfired big time. Now, the Department of Business and Innovation are using that interview as evidence I committed perjury. So, Judge, that is probably the end of my career at the Criminal Bar of England and Wales."

Looking up, I saw Judge Charles' eyes glisten. This is a man I have seen sentence people to prison for scores of years without emotion.

"Please take care of yourself, Mercer, and if I can help in any way, please let me know."
I let myself out of his room, left the courthouse, and drove once more to an empty home. I thought, *Only Vincent can help me.*

CHAPTER 15

My helper,Kasia, had left a beef stew with dumplings for me in the fridge. It only needed reheating. It was typical heavy Polish fare and it made me sleepy together with the full bottle of red I drank.

Too early to think about bed, I stretched out on the sofa. My mind was full of the wrongs done to me. Nevertheless, I managed to drop off to sleep. A sleep populated by flashbacks.

"What's up Billy-No-Mates?" asked a barrister colleague.

It was early summer 2016. I was alone at the chamber's summer garden party waiting for Claire Munro. She had called me a few days ago to tell me she had a murder brief for me – that was my first. Naturally, I was excited. She also told me she had heard about how I managed to get one of her old clients acquitted at trial. He had enthused about my skilful cross-examination of the police officer and was convinced that had secured the not guilty verdict. He was right, of course.

The art of advocacy in a criminal trial has nothing to do with the truth. Often for the defence advocate it's more a case of 'smoke and mirrors.' Advocacy is the art of storytelling and the story must be credible enough for a jury to buy so it imparts doubt upon the prosecution case. The advocate must draw out any weaknesses, usually in the form of inconsistencies, in the prosecution case.

That's what happened in the case of Claire's old client. The case against him was he was the burglar, seen inside an Islington luxury home by the homeowner. The house was under renovation at the time. The homeowner testified he was unable to identify the intruder as he only got a fleeting glimpse. But he had called the police. An officer was standing at the front door when Claire's old client, Billy, happened to descend the stairs. Billy was arrested on the more than reasonable assumption it was he who had been spotted by the homeowner on the top floor of the three-storey home.

Billy's version was that he was a building site labourer (true) and was unemployed (true). He had seen building materials outside the home and an open front door (first part true, second part possible), he decided to enter to inquire if there was any work but turned back only to be arrested, therefore the homeowner had seen an unknown person who escaped through the front door before the police arrived.

The front door had no evidence of forced entry. The key part of my cross-examination of the police officer went like this: "Officer, do you know what a climber is in police lingo?" An innocuous open question to put the officer at ease.

"Yes."

Now for the typical closed question in cross: "Would you agree with this? A climber in police vocabulary is a burglar who shimmies up buildings using fixtures like drainpipes to gain access to open windows on the upper floors of a building?"

"Yes, I agree."

Now, I can paint a picture for the jury in closing. A picture that persuades them there is a doubt. That doubt means the prosecution case is not proven to the required high standard; you must be sure before you can convict.

Sorry, I got distracted. Back to the garden party.

Still waiting, little did I know only a few hundred yards away, Claire Munro had bumped into Finbar Keogh. He had decided to leave our chamber's garden party and went to his girlfriend's chamber's garden party. She was a pupil barrister there. I was also unaware that Keogh used his Irish silver tongue to persuade Munro to give him the murder brief intended for me.

So, I'm standing there alone. My colleague was right. I'm Billy-No-Mates waiting for the murder brief that never came. The next day, Claire Munro called me to apologise. I was in no mood to accept an apology. Instead, I gave her a piece of my mind. I predicted what Keogh would do. I was right. He stole that brief to keep it from me. He knew his court diary was full. He pleaded out the murder charge by forcefully persuading the young black kid charged with murder, a carjacking gone wrong, to plead guilty to manslaughter. The kid did just that and Keogh was paid handsomely for next to no work involved.

I awoke, sweating, short of breath. There was a rage inside me. I couldn't wait for the dinner party. But would they come?

I didn't know, but the dreams continued.

.

SEVENTEEN

CHAPTER 16

There was no need to worry. Every one of them agreed to attend after I put out the word. I suspect it was a combination of the timing – a chance to go out at a quiet time of the year, and possibly curiosity as the rumours about my probable demise had started to percolate through London's legal gossip channels. The knowledge I am a good cook also helped, I'm sure, plus at one time or another I had been friends with them all. The legal fraternity possesses a communal thick skin so I'm sure not one of them thought about the real reason behind the invitation. Why should I worry? The fact was the dinner would go ahead as planned on January twenty-fifth. All I needed to do now was find a way to survive Christmas.

I had told Kasia to go home to Poland for Christmas. She was delighted, especially when I gave her a Christmas bonus of five-hundred pounds. Before she flew out of Gatwick back home to Gdansk, she called me. "Phil, are you okay left alone? I worry about you since Liz... you know, passed on. I can stay with you if you wish."

Kasia is a good-looking single lady, all of twenty-nine years old, a tall blonde with blue eyes, and legs that go on and on. It was a tempting thought, but I knew I had to prioritise my plans. "That's kind of you, but no. Please go see your family and enjoy it. Bring some vodka back though, please." I sensed her smiling,

"Okay. I will. See you second week of January."

"You will. Bye, Kasia."

It was now the eighteenth of December and I made two decisions. First, I must tee up Dave to come here for his money. That could wait until after Christmas in case he spent it all. Second thing was I vowed never to go back to work. I needed to concentrate on the other plans and make sure my affairs were in order before my almost certain imprisonment at some point after the third of February following the perjury court hearing.

A black fog of depression helped in making that decision never to return to work. I was beyond caring about income. What income? I was a self-employed barrister – no work, no pay. Anyway, I would soon be in prison. Her Majesty's Government would keep me dry, fed, and clothed. For how long I didn't know. Six months for perjury paled into insignificance compared to life for murder.

The depression told me to stay in bed, but it helped in the next few days. I kept busy ensuring I had sufficient food to last me into the New Year. Kasia had already done some shopping so I didn't have to worry about stuff men never think about until it runs out, such as toilet rolls, washing powder, dishwasher tablets, soap, toothpaste and all the other stuff the modern-day household cannot survive without.

Every morning I saw a sight that never ceased to amaze me. The postman delivered Christmas cards by the dozen. Most addressed to Mr and Mrs Mercer. That saddened me and didn't do a thing to lift the black fog. In fact, the sight of them enraged me. Not so much the remembering I was once married, but the sheer waste of money involved with people, nay sheep, bowing to the altar of commercialism. These same people who couldn't be bothered to lift a telephone to inquire about us, or me, from year to year. I guess they would justify the waste by trotting out the old line about 'I always buy charity cards,' unaware most of the money raised never ends up in charitable coffers. *Bah! Humbug*, I heard in my mind.

Christmas Eve arrived. I had my Sky cable TV subscription for company, food aplenty, and a choice of booze. No problem. I was determined to spend what was likely to be my last Christmas in my home as comfortable as possible. My only choices to make were what channel, booze, or meal should I watch, drink, or eat?

From Christmas Day onward, the depression won, not that there was any contest. It was an easy win. I stayed in bed until noon every day. No shower, no change of clothes, not for several days. Get out of bed at noon, have a pee, brush teeth, go downstairs, gaze out of the front window to check the weather, make a sandwich and coffee, turn on the TV in the kitchen, watch the news for twenty minutes, stifle a yawn, turn off TV, place dirty plate, coffee mug and utensils in the dishwasher, walk into living room, turn on the TV, select movie channel, get comfortable in my old battered leather armchair – that was my daily routine. Often, I fell asleep watching the movie. Disorientated is how I would describe feeling on waking up after those naps. I woke sweating with strong panic sensations. My stomach convulsed with a feeling of dread. My mind raced trying to fathom what I had seen in my dream. The harder I tried to recall, the white noise became louder. But something was there. I could not put my finger on it. It was impossible. Whatever it was, the something was somewhere buried deep inside of me.

EIGHTEEN

CHAPTER 17

Afghanistan 2002

My oppo hit the deck first. I followed rapidly. I didn't want to end up like the two other Brits who were now prone and lifeless a few feet in front of us. They had started to run when the ambush started. The dead Brits were suspected British born combatants who had chosen to train and fight alongside Al Qaeda. Tommy Owens, my oppo in the Intelligence Corps, and I were escorting them for questioning in an improvised interrogation centre within a British Army Forward Operating Base compound.

One of the dead suspects was a young mixed-race man who had spoken with a Birmingham accent. The other was of Pakistani appearance. He had a London accent. The two dead men and Tommy and I were all dressed similarly in adopting the local dress, wearing the knee length dress and baggy trousers known as Shalwar Kameez. All four of us also sported long beards and turbans. The dead men had naturally brown skin. As for Tommy and me, two Anglo-Saxons, the sun had darkened our complexions, made darker by rubbing earth into the skin.

I could taste the brown dirt in my mouth. I dare not spit it out. I squinted upwards towards a brilliant sun above the mountain ridges. A shape blocked the sun. I could see the silhouette of a man. He was dressed as a local Afghani like we were, but he was holding an assault rifle. We were now unarmed after we received the incoming resulting in the two dead amongst us. There had been no warning. The firefight started and was over in seconds. Tommy and I had hit the deck once we heard, "Throw down your weapons. Both of you flat out on the ground with arms outstretched above your heads." It was an American accent. I didn't know whether to relax as I thought this might be the work of the CIA. I did not trust them.

Another American accent said, "I'll blow off your freakin' heads if you make any sudden moves." Then I felt a kick in my ribs. I said nothing. The kicker rolled me over, so I was now on my back. I looked up to see a pistol pointing at my head.

The first American speaker said, "Now you. Roll over on to your back. Arms out. Let me see your hands." He kicked Tommy before he could comply. I could see he was pointing his rifle at Tommy. The second speaker was still hovering over me with the pistol aimed at my head. Tommy rolled over.

I could see the first American speaker, the one guarding Tommy, had wisps of dirty blond hair jutting out of the front of his turban. His beard was somewhat reddish. The guy holding me hostage had grey in his beard. Later, Tommy and I called them Redbeard and Greybeard but not until we were able to talk alone.

"Who are you? What you doing here?" Redbeard snapped.

I decided in an instant these guys were spooks, embedded CIA operatives. If I was wrong, we were dead.

"Mercer, Sergeant 59842109, British Army," I said sticking to protocol.

"Owens, Lance-Corporal 6545478, British Army," Tommy said.

"Who are these two ragheads?" Redbeard said, waving his rifle towards the dead men.

Tommy and I didn't answer, but the derogatory term used confirmed my gut feeling these guys were CIA.

I knew my jaw was broken as soon as I felt the blow from Redbeard's rifle butt. I felt and heard it crack. As I put my hand up to feel the jaw in a natural reflex Redbeard struck me again with his rifle butt, this time in my stomach, making me double up. Still not content, he smacked me on the back of my neck, forcing me to my knees. Who is this guy? I thought. Surely, he must be CIA or we'd both be dead by now?

Greybeard snapped plastic cuffs on our wrists once we had both been forced to stand at gunpoint, while Redbeard trained his weapon on us. Tommy and I had one arm free as they had tethered one of his wrists to mine. One the ties were secure, Redbeard, who seemed to be the leader, said, "Walk," at the same time prodding me in the back with his rifle.

We climbed as well as walked until we reached a trail up high in the mountains. The sun was setting, and the cooler air was welcome as was a gentle breeze. I knew we were heading north east because of the position of the setting sun. I thought we may be heading for Pakistan.

NINETEEN

CHAPTER 18

Present Day

Christmas had gone and I was still in the same routine and it was now the third week in January. Only seven days to go before the dinner party. Note to self – *snap out of it!* Luckily, I knew exactly how to do that – get busy, that was how. I think having Kasia back helped too. I didn't want her to see me wandering around my home looking and smelling like a dishevelled smelly tramp.

I gave her the shopping list for all the ingredients I would need except for the belly pork. I would select that myself. I also needed to buy a few props needed for the parlour game I had planned. I knew I could find them in Brixton market. It was vital she wouldn't be here when I killed my guests. I didn't need complications. I got around that by giving her clear instructions. She was to answer the door to all my guests, take their coats, place them in the living room over the back of the sofa, then seat them at the dining table. Once seated, she would serve an expensive champagne before she left to go home. I would be cooking with my back to my guests. Of course, I would chat to them, but they would be staring at my back. Besides, they could see I was busy, and I would encourage them to chat amongst themselves until dinner was served. *Tra-la!* I thought, *Perfecto!*

Once Kasia left that day, I started having doubts once more. *Can I truly commit murder? Am I capable?*

It was at these times of uncertainty that Vincent would appear. I'd not heard or seen him since before Christmas. I was beginning to miss him... a little.

"You can. You must," Vincent said.

I heard him but no one was there.

The fresh air felt and smelled good. I had been too long cooped up at home. The changes in my daily habits no doubt helped. I was cleaner and felt it too. I also wore clean clothes, casual but smart. Not too smart, mind, as I knew I would be tramping around some of the dodgier parts of Brixton market, the narrow paths under the railway arches. The parts the cops dare not venture. That's where you find weed, crack cocaine, and other illegal wares, if you were that way minded. Nothing I planned to buy was illegal. A new sharp butcher's cleaver, for instance. It's not illegal *per se*. It is if you intend to use it as an offensive weapon, which I did, but only Vincent seemed to know my thoughts. *My thoughts? Or are they Vincent's? Who is he?*

My other port of call would be a pet shop. They sell nothing illegal at all that I'm aware of. The usual crew was lining the narrow passages separating the stalls under the arches. "Weed, man?" was the sales pitch from one skinny young Rasta in an affected Jamaican Patois. They weren't all young but all were black, probably all first or second generation British-born of parents who emigrated to Britain from the Caribbean in the 1950s. I knew from experience the best bet was to ignore these calls to buy, and all eye contact, best to walk by briskly as if one belonged. In contrast, the unwary white-skinned visitor to Brixton was often robbed at knifepoint because they acted and looked like victims. The 'crew' threw me some quizzical looks when I stopped to purchase my meat cleaver at the last stall. I ignored it all and kept to my urban survival rulebook. If they had followed me to the pet shop, they would have been even more curious. It was late afternoon and time to go home.

The house was warm when I walked into the hall. I'd left the heating on the all-day setting. After removing my coat and NY Yankees baseball hat, I set about stowing away my purchases. First, I went to the kitchen, unwrapped the cleaver and placed it in a drawer but not before gingerly running my finger along the chopping edge. *That'll work*, I thought. *Hmm, where should I keep the box from the pet shop?* Before taking it somewhere safe and warm, I made some extra puncture holes in the main box and the smaller ones contained inside. *Don't want the buggers to die*, I was thinking as I made my way to their temporary home. "Now, stay there until I need you," I said, patting the box.

Once I'd got that out of the way, I called Dave's mobile. "Yes, I have the cash. Can you come here, say in an hour?"

One hour and ten minutes later, the doorbell rang. On opening the front door, I saw Dave in t-shirt and jeans. "Bit cold to be dressed like that," I observed.

He turned his head to the road outside in the direction of a parked car with its engine running. I could see the exhaust fumes in the red glow thrown out by the car's rear lights. "Nah," he said, "my mate gave me a lift. Didn't want to carry all that cash around with me. Too many thieves out there," he added with a cheeky Cockney chuckle.

"Okay, makes sense, I guess. Come in."

Dave followed me into the hall after he signalled his mate in the car by raising all five fingers of one hand, a universal sign language for 'I'll be back in five.' I took him through to the dining room cum kitchen. Gesturing for him to take a seat at the table, I pulled out a padded envelope from a kitchen drawer. Handing it to Dave, I said, "Better count it. Thirty thousand in total bundled into five thousand each pile." Most were in fifty-pound denominations with twenties making up about twenty percent of the total and tenners about five percent.

"Thanks, Mister... I mean Phil. I think it may take me longer than five minutes."

"Take your time."

Dave broke off from counting. "These fifties are kosher, right?"

"Course, why do you ask?"

"I read about a trial you did over at Snaresbrook. A big forgery trial, making fifty-pound notes, they was. I laughed when I read you had the Bank of England expert all tied up in knots."

I recalled it. Dave was right. My client, the ring-leader's daughter, put forward the case she had never operated the film-stamping machine essential for stamping the metal strips on to the paper to make the notes appear authentic. Police surveillance videos showed her coming in and out of her home when she was supposed to be operating the machine, according to the prosecution. The success of her defence rested on how much time was required to operate the machine.

The expert conceded to me in cross-examination he had never tested it, so he was unable to say how much time was required. The jury acquitted my client.

Dave added, "These bullseyes ain't from that case, is they?"

"Bullseyes?"

"C'mon. Cockney for fifty."

"Oh, right. No, they are legit. I got them from the bank a few days ago."

"That's okay then. Can I ask you something?"

"Sure, go ahead."

"You sure you want me to plant these bombs?"

"I'm sure, yes."

"That's good because I tested that stuff last week. I wanted to see what it would do to reinforced concrete and how much to use."

"Bloody hell, Dave. Where was this?"

"In the mountains in Wales. Not a soul around for miles unless you count sheep."

"And... what happened?"

"There was an abandoned house. Mostly it was falling to pieces with no roof. But it has a couple of concrete pillars still standing. Or it did. I blew one up. Worked a treat."

"You used the mobile phone to detonate it?"

"Yeah, connected it to the detonator. Packed it all into a hole I made and then from half a mile away I used one of the other phones to detonate the thing. Boom! I saw it. Tell you the truth, I enjoyed it."

"Great work. Don't forget the twenty-fifth, will you?"

"The twenty-fifth?"

"That's the night you need to do it. Ten at night, okay?"

"No problem. Fuck this counting. I trust you. My mate will be getting shirty waiting outside."

Dave stuffed the banknotes into the envelope, and I let him out of the front door.

A mixture of relief and fear swept over me. *What AM I doing?* Opening a bottle of red, I turned on the TV news channel. Up popped a news report about US soldiers in Afghanistan. I could hear someone off camera talking in Pashto. What's more, I thought for one moment I could understand.

Pashto! How the hell would I know any Pashto? I dozed off on the sofa thinking of

Pashto and one name kept flashing through my mind – *Vincent.*

TWENTY

CHAPTER 19

Afghanistan 2002

My jaw throbbed with every step I took so I was relieved when the two Americans pointed to a cave.

"We rest up in there for the night," Redbeard said. Tommy looked glum. I almost remonstrated with him but decided to keep schtum. The less we said, the less chance of the Yanks beating us. Tommy is one of the few people I can bollock and he doesn't take it personally. He knows I do it for his own good. We are like brothers. We look out for each other. That's not just because we are in the same mob. We went through basic together and got to

know each other well. Then much to each other's delight, we went on the same language courses: German, Russian, and Pashto. The Pashto is why we were deployed in the field in Afghanistan. The Russian came in handy too, as some of the older Mujahedeen knew some Russian. Besides all that, he's solid and a good soldier too. I believe he thinks of me like I do him. The one thing that pisses me off about him is his Welshness. To be exact, the ability to switch rapidly from elation to despair. Quite a few of the Taffs I know are the same.

The cave was dry. I could see that but little else as it was now pitch-black outside. I didn't think they would light a fire. It was too risky up in the mountains. Whoever these Americans were, they were as welcome as we were to bandits, not to mention Al Qaeda or the Taliban. We were all intruders. But I didn't know what game these Yanks were playing. I thought they were CIA the more I observed them. They had a gung-ho attitude like regular soldiers but seemed to lack discipline. I didn't believe they were special forces either, because of the giveaways in their manner of dress. Looking at us two, at first and second glance, we could pass off as Afghani locals, not them. They wore expensive sunglasses, high-end wrist watches, branded jeans and footwear. They also smoked American branded cigarettes. The thing I noticed, or felt, was they were sinister. I knew no good was going to come of this involuntary excursion. We were prisoners, but why and where were we heading?

Redbeard broke my thought train. I heard, "Here, eat this." He threw us some dry field rations. Reaching into his backpack again, he flung a flask. "Water," was all he said.

I needed that water to eat the food. If food was what you could call it. It was like a dry pitta bread sandwich filled with some unidentifiable paste. It all came wrapped in a sealed pouch. Tommy was ahead of me. He knew I would have trouble opening the pouch, so he took mine and bit the package open before handing me the contents and water. I took a mouthful of water and used it to soften the rations, making it easier for me to swallow as my jaw was still painful, but it helped.

Twenty yards separated us from our two captors. We were still tethered to each other. I was ready for sleep despite the pain in my jaw and almost grateful when Redbeard said, "Lights out. Don't get any ideas. One of us will be watching you. If you make any moves at all, we will kill you."

I dared to ask, "Any blankets?" It was cold.

"Yes, we have. You two will have to keep each other warm."

Clearly, Greybeard was the joker. "Cuddle up, boys. But remember no sex before marriage." I heard both laugh quietly.

"Fuck you," was what I wanted to say but said nothing.

Tommy and I got as comfortable as best we could. I lay on my right side to avoid any pressure to my jaw. One of my wrists was tied to Tommy's wrist so he wriggled about to accommodate me in getting as comfortable as possible. I have no clue how I managed to sleep with Tommy close to my back, but we were kept warm. I recall thinking before I dropped off that these Americans were weird. I didn't like them one bit. It scared me wondering what the hell was in store for us. They seemed like a couple of psychos.

TWENTY-ONE

CHAPTER 20

Present Day

Sleep wasn't a problem most nights. I dropped off okay but there were many lurid dreams, and they were becoming more vivid. Sometimes, I'd wake up from one of them utterly convinced it wasn't a dream at all. I think I was reliving something from my past. That's the trouble; *I think but I don't know.*

There was an itch somewhere at the back of my mind and I couldn't scratch it. I also had the classic chase dreams. Once I was so scared, I jumped to escape… in my dream, but woke up covered in blood from a cut on my forehead. I had leapt from bed, landing on the corner of a bedside cabinet. I had dreams about Liz, too. That was weird because they were true and like watching an old movie where I knew every single line of dialogue, or at least the dramatic bits. The one I recall best was after I had been demobbed... back to Civvy Street, and she had to remind me where we first met. Now that is strange, me not recalling where I met the love of my life. I never forgot our anniversary, mind you, there was a framed wedding photo with the date in the corner of the image.

My waking hours were spent scheming. I was planning the events of this coming Saturday right down to the fine details. It was now Friday the twenty-fourth, only one day to go. Kasia doesn't normally work on Saturdays but she agreed to help on this occasion, especially since there was an extra cash bonus involved. I'm sure she got tired of me going over her part as I once saw her sigh when I repeated her instructions for the fifth time that day. Was it a sigh? Yes, it was, along with the 'whatever' raised eyebrows look.

After she left, I set about preparing the belly pork so next day I could pop it into the oven. It would need about six hours in there to ensure there was a crispy, dark brown crackling. I swear I started salivating at the thought of eating the crispy skin.

Opening a bottle of red, I poured myself a large glass then set out all the ingredients on the worktop next to the large cutting board. First, I retrieved the belly pork from the refrigerator, setting it down on a large plate. It was a boneless rind-on cut, about ten pounds in weight. Reaching up to my herb rack, I grabbed the small jar of whole black peppercorns and sea salt, setting them down within easy reach. Next was my mortar and pestle to crush the whole fennel seeds, part of a deseeded red bell pepper, fresh rosemary, thyme leaves, and a few garlic cloves.

Heaving the roasting tray from the oven, I trimmed and squared off the pork belly to fit the tray. The meat was then placed skin-side down on the cutting board. Using a sharp chef's knife, I scored the flesh at an angle using strokes about one inch apart. Then rotating the knife at ninety degrees, I repeated it to create a diamond pattern in the flesh. That was when I thought about Hannibal Lecter, or rather Anthony Hopkins who played the part. I started to imagine him cutting human flesh. Strange!

Concentrating once more, I got the small frying pan in which I toasted the peppercorns and fennel seeds until lightly browned and could smell the aroma, that took about two minutes. I transferred that to the mortar and pestle and ground until roughly crushed. Then I mixed in the salt, red pepper, herbs and garlic to form a dry rub. I used my hands to rub the mixture deep into the cracks and crevices in the meat. This is going to be delicious. I really don't think I could eat human flesh no matter how it was cooked.

The tricky part was next. I rolled the meat into a tight log and placed it seam-side down on top of the cutting board. Using some kitchen twine cut long enough to tie around the pork I lay them down in regular intervals along my cutting board, about one-inch apart. Then I lay the rolled pork seam-side down on top of the strings. Once done, I tied up the roast tightly. Finally, I mixed the sea salt with one teaspoon of baking powder and rubbed that over the entire surface of the pork roast. It was now ready for overnight in the fridge, so I wrapped the *porchetta* tightly in plastic and popped it into the refrigerator. I took one final glance as the fridge light came on. It almost looked like a severed arm. As that thought came into my head, I heard the white noise again but louder. I need to chill out.

I poured myself another glass of red. Turning on the kitchen TV, I settled into one of the dining room carver chairs. I didn't watch what was showing. My eyes were drawn to my armoury – the meat cleaver, and assorted knives. *Things will soon get bloody,* I thought.

Before retiring to bed later that evening I checked on my 'box of tricks' – my surprises I had bought at the market for my guests. All was good.

TWENTY-TWO

CHAPTER 21

While Mercer busied himself in the kitchen with final culinary preparations, Kasia followed her instructions to the letter. All the guests arrived within thirty minutes of each other. The solicitors, Claire Munro and Diedre Summers, were first to arrive, having shared a black cab. Mercer heard their noisy arrival as Kasia took their coats and led them to the dining table for champagne. Must have been drinking already, Mercer thought, listening to the cackling. "Had a loosener or two on the way?" he said.

"A cheeky little drink or three, yes. In the Dog and Pheasant, you remember it, don't you, Phil? From our uni days," Munro said.

"I do." Mercer also thought, and that's why you are here.

Mercer turned to face them. "Sorry, ladies. Please let me finish the prep. When all is ready, we can eat and talk. I'm looking forward to it."

He could see their faces clearly but felt confused as he seemed to be looking through a narrow tube. Everything, other than their faces, was blurred. Turning away from his guests he started to walk to the far side of the kitchen but felt unsteady on his feet. He stumbled but held on to the kitchen worktop to regain balance.

One by one his guests were seated at the table. Kasia filled their champagne flutes and left the opened bottle in a large ice bucket in the middle of the table. She also advised them to permit Mercer to work uninterrupted until he was ready to serve.

Mercer was delighted with Kasia's intuitive intervention. This was not on the instructions list. He carried on working with his final preparations – vegetables including red peppers, red onion, butternut squash, baby leeks, courgettes, an aubergine, and two tomatoes plus some cloves of garlic. The pork belly porchetta with crispy skin had been in the oven for hours.

He could hear the conversation behind him in the room. He recognised all the voices, identifying them in his head. There were six besides the two solicitors who arrived first together: Piers Allen, Lucy Fairweather, David Ramsbottom and Finbar Keogh, all barristers, and Brad Collins, the Senior Clerk. Mercer smiled deep inside at the knowledge all of them would die. No sooner had the smile radiated throughout his whole being, he sensed fear. I can't do this, he thought. As much as they wronged me, I can't kill them.

"You can and you must," someone said. Mercer heard it. Watching his hands paring vegetables,

his gaze fell upon a face. It was there in the middle of the discarded vegetable peelings.

"Vincent!" Mercer cried. The room fell silent. He was expecting someone to say something, but no one commented on his outcry. The normal conversational hubbub started up once more. Am I slowly going mad? Mercer thought.

Mercer opened the double oven to check on the pork belly. Withdrawing the large roasting tray, he knew it needed another thirty minutes or so at a higher temperature to crisp the outside to perfection. He calculated cooking times in his head. Fifteen minutes more for the pork to rest, he thought. Mercer placed the prepared vegetables in a second smaller roasting tray, seasoned them with ground black pepper, sea salt, ground coriander seeds, rosemary and thyme before drizzling virgin olive oil over the vegetables. Job done, he placed that in the separate pre-heated oven and set the timer for forty-five minutes before he spoke to Kasia.

"Kasia, you're all done now. Thank you."

"I can stay a while longer if you like, Mister Mercer."

"No, I can do the rest."

He thought, Go before there's bloody mayhem. His attention drifted back to the oven, thinking he'd never noticed the loose control knob before. This is crazy, or is it me who's mad? I'm going to murder these people and I let a loose knob distract me? he thought.

Mercer saw Kasia to the front door. Opening it, she said, "The food smells wonderful. And you know what... it makes sure your guests can't smell that disgusting sewer odour."

"That's true, I hadn't thought about it until now."

"Bye. I hope all goes well. See you Monday."

Mercer locked the front door behind her before returning to his guests. His peripheral vision still blanked out, he made for the direction of the light escaping from the open door leading to the kitchen cum dining room, steadying himself to avoid any more stumbles.

Joining his guests at the table, he picked up a champagne flute at his place setting. "Who's going to fill this?" He needed some help with that simple task owing to his tunnel vision. Claire poured his champagne.

Returning to her seat, she said, "Phil, I had no idea you were a chef. If it tastes as good as it smells, yummy is all I can say."

Mercer ignored her. The dinner table conversation continued without him. He was there in body, but his mind was elsewhere. He felt it all was surreal as if he were in the middle of a Salvador Dali painting.

TWENTY-THREE

CHAPTER 22

"Phil, what can I say? The food was delightful,"
Diedre said.

Mercer heard both Keogh and Allen chime in,
"Hear, hear."

"Glad you enjoyed it. Now can someone do me a
favour, please?"

"Sure," Collins said, "what do you want?"

"Clear the table of all the dirty dishes. Load the
dishwasher, and let's get some serious drinking
done." His guests knew nothing of his visual
impairment. "There are fresh glasses up there in

that cabinet. Red wine over there," fingers pointing at the locations, "white plonk in that small fridge below the counter. The red I can recommend. As for the white, I haven't got a clue. It's probably anti-freeze."

Claire laughed her girly giggle. "Still got a sense of humour, I see."

"Of course." Mercer smiled his trademark lopsided grin.

"I know you used to get huffy with me when I used to mention your lopsided grin. But you know what? It's actually quite attractive. I bet juries love the look," Deirdre said.

"As long as they don't think I'm Drew Barrymore in drag, I guess you could be right. Juries do like me for the most part. I mean, you can't win 'em all over can you? What's up, Deirdre? Can you now see you just might have made a mistake in not instructing me for some of those libel cases?"

Collins and Diedre did the chores. Probably the two biggest alcoholics, Mercer thought.

Mercer found by swivelling his head slowly he could manage to see everyone one at a time in the light at the end of the tunnel. Their features blocked out the bright light behind them. Piers Allen was the easiest to fix because he was sat opposite Mercer.

Satisfied all were now settled at the table with drinks in front of them, Mercer said, "Are you all comfortable? Have you all got a drink?" He didn't want any interruptions.

"Yes, go on," Allen said as if he were spokesperson for all.

Pompous twat! Mercer thought. It's not what he says, it's the way he says it. You might be first to die.

"I have this idea. It will be fun. Like a parlour game."

"Like charades?" Deirdre said.

"Not exactly, no. It's a 'storytelling game.'"

"Is that fair?" Collins said.

"What do you mean?" Mercer said.

"Most of you at the table are barristers. Storytelling, eloquence and ease of articulating yourselves are essential to your roles as advocates. Even the two solicitors, Claire and Deidre, have some advocacy experience."

"It's a game, not a competition. There's no prizes. It's for fun. To make it even more fun, the easy choice is not an option at all. What terrifies you? What scares you shitless? Be brave. Be reckless. You are among friends. What can possibly go wrong? It's just a parlour game, right?"

TWENTY-FOUR

CHAPTER 23

A silence hung over the room until Claire Munro spoke. "It sounds like fun to me. Let's do it. Do you have a name for this game?"

"Comfort zone."

"Super name! You should patent it."

"If that were possible, I would." Let's get on with this, thought Mercer. Not one of them has asked how I am. They all knew about Liz's death even if they don't yet know about my brush with the law and my imminent court appearance. Selfish people! Kill them!

"Shut up, Vincent!"

"Steady on, old chap. No need to shout, and who the heck is Vincent?" David Ramsbottom said.

"What are you talking about?"

"You just shouted, 'Shut up, Vincent!'"

"I did?"

"Yes," Mercer heard Diedre say somewhere over to his right. He felt the room start to sway like he was aboard a boat in a rolling sea.

Piers Allen ignored all this. "Okay, I'll go first. First, let me say advocacy is a form of storytelling. It has nothing to do with the truth. In a criminal trial, the aim is to set up the ducks, as it were, in the prosecution case, then shoot them down one by one. One doesn't have to shoot them dead. Injure them, seriously injure them, will suffice. Then, when it comes for me to deliver my final speech to the jury, I can demolish the credibility of the prosecution case duck by duck. Quack, quack. Not guilty, members of the jury."

Mercer saw Allen's chest swell with pride, or was it conceit? Mercer thought, quickly intervening. "Piers, thank you for volunteering, but I would hate your advocacy skills to intimidate those less confident of their own abilities. I suggest one of Brad, Claire or Deidre go first. Volunteers?"

Brad Collins, the Senior Clerk piped up. "Pour me one of those malts you have up there and I'll give it a go." A short pause followed. Mercer guessed correctly someone was doing as Collins asked. He heard the man take a gulp of his golden smooth whisky before saying, "Right. Here's what really scares me. I would hate to be poor."

"Is that it?" Mercer asked. "I mean... where's the story?"

"I'm no good at story telling."

"Look, Brad. This is a game. Give it a go. Why would you hate to be poor? Why does that scare you?"

"Okay, but some of this is personal so please respect that."

"Don't worry, Brad, what goes on in Phil's kitchen stays in Phil's kitchen," Claire said.

TWENTY-FIVE

CHAPTER 24

Collins continued, "You lot are all educated professionals. Me? I'm only a product of the East End, born and raised in Bow. I still live there. Like a lot of barristers' clerks, I'm not much more than a glorified barrow boy at heart. A costermonger. That's what I did at first on leaving school at fifteen. It was my father's fruit and veg stall at Walthamstow market. His father before him also operated the stall. My mother used to help out too until she got sick. It was then my old man started gambling. He'd use the takings to bet on horses, dogs, you name it. He lost everything and was eventually made bankrupt. We got evicted because the bank repossessed our house. That was it for Mum, she died soon after.

"A mate of mine told me about a vacancy as a clerk in a barristers' chambers. I applied and got the job. The rest, as they say, is history. That's why being poor frightens me. I never want what happened to my Dad happen to me."

I feel sorry for him, Mercer thought. I can't kill him. "Sad story, Brad. I didn't know your history. Claire, you want to go next?" *he said.*

"Why not?" she said, first taking a huge gulp of white wine. "Snakes. Not the human sort who are usually men, by the way. I can deal with them. I have a phobia about the slithery ones. You know, the ones that go, 'Hiss.' Snakes on a Plane, *that's one film I just cannot watch. I can't even watch* Jungle Book *and that's a cartoon. They give me the creeps and as for the ones with flicking tongues and the hood, what are they called?"*

"Cobras," Piers Allen said.

"Yeah, cobras. I think I'd rather be killed any other way but by a snake. Horrible, slimy things."

"Phil, do you mind if I go now? I'm the same as Claire, but spiders not snakes. I can't watch anything to do with spiders. If I see one, I freak out endlessly. I'm shaking now at the thought of the horrible hairy beasts. I mean... what the fuck is the point of them?" Deirdre said.

David Ramsbottom intervened. "This isn't storytelling. Brad was at least honest enough to tell us why he had a fear of poverty. You two," pointing at Clare Munro and Deirdre Summers, "merely tell us what frightens you. That's not the game as I understand it. Is that right, Phil?" He sat back, preening his moustache.

"Correct, but no worries, I'm sure us advocates can comply and entertain. Why don't you go next, David?" Mercer said.

"I will and please don't interrupt or laugh. I have an insatiable sexual appetite. I do think it's a

psychological issue. In fact, I know so. I underwent therapy with a Harley Street psychologist. The trouble was she was a woman… a sexy woman. She explored the reasons behind my… shall we say… unusually high sex drive. Apparently, it stemmed from my lack of height. Subconsciously, I was always trying to prove myself both between the sheets and in my profession.

"After a few sessions, she decided to discuss the size of my member. I assured her there was no problem in that department. Well, and this is all true, she was one of these avant-garde new wave of sex therapists so wasn't averse to getting down to business if you know what I mean. She produced a condom. I got hard. She rolled it on my dick, and we fucked.

"I paid for another few sessions but carried on seeing her for months after they ended. We had sex twice a week every which way, the whole Kama Sutra *thing. It all ended after her husband found*

out and he killed her. So, the thing that scares me most is becoming impotent."

"No sign of that, David. I know you have a hard on for me. I also know that's why you wanted me as your junior on that murder trial up in Lancashire and not Phil," said Lucy Fairweather. "Phil, do you mind if I give this game a miss?"

Thank goodness, Mercer thought. I might spare you.

"That's fine, Lucy," Mercer said, noting her lack of usual aggression. In fact, Mercer thought she looked lifeless, almost like a corpse. Her usual energy had disappeared. She was speaking in monotone and dressed head to foot in black. No sooner had he thought this than he dismissed the ludicrous notion she was already dead.

"Fin?" Mercer queried, switching his attention to Finbar Keogh.

"Right you are, " Keogh said in his Ulster lilt. "It's an open secret I'm gunning for silk. I know I'm ruthless in that aim and I won't be any different until I have the letters Q.C. behind my name. Sounds good, don't you think? Finbar Keogh, Queen's Counsel.

"A bit like David here, but a different kind of impotence, I never wish to lose my ruthless edge. That's what scares me most. Ruthlessness tends to be despised and I don't understand why. Sometimes, even after you've exhausted all options. Even after you've tried everything to make it right. Even after you've stood your ground time and time again, you're still going to run into characters who just don't see it any other way than their own. What's there left to do? Unfortunately, sometimes you must play dirty too. There's no room left to be civilised. All bets are off when you've tried playing kind and fair and you keep getting knocked down, each time getting worse. Now, you must be ruthless. Desperate times call for desperate measures. I tried all that nicey-nicey

stuff when I first started practice at the Bar. I soon realised that was not enough to reach my ultimate goals.

"It doesn't feel good when someone lets you down, promises are broken. It gets worse if you feel pinned into a corner and helpless. You have no idea when the next cheque will arrive. You have nowhere to turn to, nothing left to do, so fighting fire with fire might just be the only way there is to go. What would you do? Be nice and poor or ruthless and succeed?"

"Okay. Time for Piers to close the game. You all okay with that?" Mercer said.

"What about you, Phil?" one voice asked.

"Don't worry, I'll do my party piece at the end. Piers, don't forget the rules now, will you? What terrifies you?"

"I have to say that involves anything to spoil my youthful good looks."

Yeah, pompous and conceited, thought Mercer. The host could see Allen's face clearly in the middle of his tunnel vision. Stretching a little to his right, Mercer picked up a glass bottle hidden under a napkin. Unscrewing the top, he threw the contents at Allen's smirking face.

Allen's shriek was ungodly. All present at the table saw Allen's face dissolve in wisps of vapour accompanied by the sight of skin falling away and the acrid smell of burning flesh. Mercer saw only Allen's facial bones, even his nose had melted. The sight fascinated him. That'll wipe the smirk off your face, Mercer thought before he said, "What's up, old chap, your bloated ego unable to cope with a loss of face?" Mercer roared at his own witticism.

Claire Munro shouted, "You are stark raving mad! Bonkers!"

"Maybe. I don't care what you think. Soon you will all be dead."

TWENTY-SIX

CHAPTER 25

"Why? For god's sake, why?" Claire screamed.

"Why? Why? Where do I start? I know. Not one of you self-centred pieces of shit has ever asked me how I am. I lost my wife, my mother, my brother and am about to lose my livelihood. What the fuck is wrong with you all? I'll go around the room and tell you all individually just why you're going to die.

"Before I do, that's too late for smarmy Piers there. He was an asshole extraordinaire. He went around telling clients not to trust me because I used to be a cop which, by the way, was entirely

false. But the damage was done in some quarters. That's count one in the charges of depriving me of income. His only assets were his boyish good looks. Well, look at him now. He has no face at all.

"Count two is you, Claire. We were such close friends at uni. Where was the work I rightly expected coming from you? Yes. A couple of cases and successful outcomes but you were too busy shagging detectives who sent clients your way, not to mention shagging the young barristers who took your fancy. 'Ooh, nice fuck and here's a brief or three as a thank you. Please fuck me again.' I can hear you saying that as I speak.

"Then to top it all was the day of the chamber's garden party. You called me to tell me you were bringing over a murder brief. I was delighted. I waited and waited but you never showed up. Instead, you were seduced by the golden Irish tongue of good old Finbar here. Instead of the boy getting unbiased counsel's advice, what happened? Keogh pleaded it out. That's count

three. He did it not because it was the right thing to do but because his fucking diary was too full to accommodate the trial. So, rather than pass it over, preferably to me where it belonged, he did the ruthless thing he's so good at. Well, I have news for Finbar Keogh, he will never have the letters Q.C. behind his name.

"Count four, Deidre, you were so wrong about those libel cases. At least you could have tried me out perhaps as a junior with leading counsel. But, no, Deirdre knew best. In fact, the truth is Deirdre knows fuck all about advocacy. You get off on the power you wield over barristers.

"Count five, Brad, I'm sort of sorry having to kill you. Your story in the game tonight moved me. Your fear of poverty, though, had an undesirable effect on my income. Your greed affected me. You switched briefs and some big-earning briefs willy-nilly to the top bidder. If not for your corruption, I may have been able to settle things with the

bankruptcy. The interview with the Insolvency Service would never have happened.

"Count six is reserved for you, David. You were the biggest contributor to Brad's secret slush fund. As the smallest barrister in chambers you had to find a way of grabbing cases that gave you that sense of aggrandisement. You weren't content with that, but also extended your influence to selecting who should be your junior on the biggest fee-earning cases. That, in the case of Lucy, was made not on the basis of ability but driven by your sexual predatory instincts.

"Lucy, be honest, did you ever sleep with David?"

"Once."

"Your life hangs in the balance. Answer this truthfully. Has he a big one or a small one?"

"Well, Phil, I suppose four inches is quite big for such a small man."

"Size is relative, I guess," Mercer said.

Sensing he had a captive audience, Mercer decided to delay the executions for a while. I'm enjoying this, he thought, and I may as well get a lot more off my chest.

He heard Vincent. "Attaboy, Phil."

"Listen, this is for the benefit of those who don't know, like you, Claire and you, Deirdre. It's also for the rest who should have known better. Have you any idea what it's like trying to build a practice at the Criminal Bar?

"Unless you are lucky enough to have had a privileged background, gone to Eton, got a first at Oxford, joined an elite set of posh boy barristers who do little else than nab all the cream cases, then it's a struggle. You need at least half a dozen well-paying cases a year. That may mean you receive one hundred thousand in income, but that's not all yours. We are independent self-employed practitioners, so first, we have to pay taxes. Then there are the deductions for chambers' rent, the clerks' fees and so on. If you want to plan

ahead, you need to pay into a pension scheme. There is no sick pay so if you don't work you get no money. Travel expenses, the purchase of law books, an occasional new suit for court. They all add up. Not to mention shoes – there's more walking involved than many people realise, especially in London; bus, tube, train, walk to the courthouse.

"To make matters worse, the legal aid cuts have made it harder than ever to earn a decent crumb. I don't blame the government though, it was the likes of David who milked the old system. In their day they even referred to it as the gravy train. It was money for old rope. So, out of what's left you have a mortgage to pay and other household bills. I'm glad Liz and I had no kids because a private education would have been out of the question.

"Anyway, it's now time for your deaths, but first, Claire, here is a surprise for you."

Mercer opened the box. "How do you like that, Claire?" He threw the cobra at her. It landed in front of her, flicking its fangs in and out, hood out, and ready to strike. She fainted. "Deirdre, I have something for you too," he said as he opened another box containing a large tarantula. He tossed it and the box across the dining table towards her. She screamed.

"Don't worry, the snake and the spider had their venom removed. The look on your faces has made my day."

Mercer's vision had now returned but the room was spinning out of control. It rocked from left to right, then back again. He went to the worktop to fetch the meat cleaver. Turning around, he saw all his guests, except the dead Piers Allen, looking terrified. Steadying himself, he chopped and slashed. One by one, he maimed them. Arms were severed, hands chopped off, necks struck with mortal blows. Blood sprayed from arteries, flowed from veins until no blood was left. They were all dead.

"Good man. I knew you had it in you." Mercer heard Vincent's voice. The room had stopped rocking.

"Better clean it all up tomorrow before Kasia gets here on Monday," Mercer said chuckling like a maniac.

He felt the chuckle turning into a deep belly laugh when he felt his breath sucked out of his chest. It felt like an excruciating blast of scorching air lasting for only milliseconds, but he knew it was extremely hot because he couldn't breathe. He also saw a starburst of brilliant white light. The parlour game was over.

TWENTY-SEVEN

CHAPTER 26

"Mister Mercer, Phillip, can you hear me?"

On looking up, I saw a young woman dressed in a nurse's uniform. I felt frightened to ask any questions in case I was dead.

My mouth was as dry as the Sahara, but I mumbled, "I can hear you."

"Good. The doctor will come to see you soon. He will explain everything. You have a visitor too. He has been here at least three times, but you were still in a coma. He'll be delighted to see you later. Brad Collins is his name. Said he is a professional acquaintance of yours. I take it you do know him?"

"I do, yes. Is he okay?"

"What?"

"Was he hurt too?"

The nurse's brow furrowed. At first, I thought she was about to deliver bad news but then it dawned on me – it was a look of puzzlement.

"Please don't worry yourself and wait for the doctor. She won't be long."

"Where am I?"

"St. Thomas's Hospital."

"In London?"

"Yes."

"So, I'm not dead?"

"Not yet, no, and if we have anything to do with it, you should live to a ripe old age."

Waiting for the doctor to arrive, I saw my left arm was in a plaster cast. That made me check out the rest of me. I wriggled the toes of both feet, followed up by a tentative knees-bend. Wonderful! No pain and all body parts were working. What the hell happened? The nurse mentioned coma. A broken arm doesn't do that. I could see I was in a ward, but my thoughts were interrupted by the swish of the privacy curtain pulled around my bed.

A slim, dark-haired woman dressed in a white doctor's coat peered over her spectacles at me. Clearing her throat, she said, "How are you feeling?"

"Mouth's dry and my head feels fuzzy. Apart from that, I feel okay."

"No headache?"

"No."

"Good. We'll keep you in for one more night for observations. If you still feel okay tomorrow, we can discharge you."

"Doctor?"

"Yes?"

"Do you mind telling me what happened?"

"You suffered a severe concussion resulting in a brain haematoma, a swelling of the brain. The surgeon induced a coma to increase your chances of the swelling receding. We monitored you closely, of course. That was in ICU, then moved on to this ward to recover."

"The arm?"

"Forgive me, I should have explained. There was an explosion at your home. A natural gas explosion. It seems you had a leak at the connection from the mains to the central heating boiler. The police will want to ask you some questions about that in case it was faulty workmanship."

"So, I broke my arm and hit my head hard on something, is that what you are saying happened?"

"Yes, it appears so."

"How is it I didn't get killed if it was an explosion?"

"Natural gas explosions don't occur very often. When they do, the building is destroyed. The roof inevitably disappears but fatalities are rare. I'm sure the police will answer those questions fully and they will also have the reports of the Fire Brigade and Health and Safety investigations."

"How long have I been in hospital?"

"Four days now. You were admitted on Friday night."

"Friday. You mean Saturday, surely?"

"Friday, Mister Mercer. How could we forget? Four explosions in the same evening. One in Islington, two in Holborn and your home in Brixton. The other three were deliberate. Someone set off bombs inside the buildings. You see the man three beds down?"

"Yes."

"He was passing by, walking his dog, when he was knocked over by some flying masonry. Like you, he suffered a severe concussion and ended up here."

The man was prone in his hospital bed. I guess he was recovering, like me.

'Anyway, enough talk from me. The nurses will continue to monitor you until I do my rounds tomorrow morning. All being well, we can discharge you then. A social worker will come to see you to find out where you can stay."

"Thanks, Doctor."

TWENTY-EIGHT

CHAPTER 27

About one hour later, the same nurse approached my bed. "Your visitor is here again, Mr Collins. Do you feel up to seeing him?"

"Yes, I feel okay."

Before leaving to bring Brad Collins to my bed, she helped me to sit upright, plumping the pillows behind me in support of my back. I felt apprehensive but decided to play it all by ear.

"Phil," Brad gasped. "How are you? I have tried to get to see you a few times now."

"I'll survive, according to the doctor. In fact, I'm told I may be out tomorrow."

"That is great news. I thought you were a goner when I saw the devastation the blast had caused."

"Blast?"

"Your home, Phil, don't you know what happened?"

"Not really. I was told by the doctor it was a gas explosion."

"That's right, or that's what the authorities are saying. It's been all over the news. A gas leak, apparently. You were lucky to survive."

"Must have been when Liz arranged for the new central heating boiler. He must have fucked up the pipe connections, I guess."

"That's what the fire brigade and the health and safety are saying. The police have arrested a guy for manslaughter."

"Manslaughter? I'm alive, or so I was told."

"Your next-door neighbour was killed. The blast ripped away part of next door, too. The pictures were all over the BBC news. It looked like a World War Two scene."

I fell silent, taking in all this new information.

"Phil? Are you okay?"

"Fine, fine. Just taking in the enormity of it all. I suppose it was a blessing it all happened the day before my planned dinner party."

"As it turned out we couldn't have gone anyway."

"Why?"

"Chambers was bombed the same night. Claire Munro's office too, or I should say, where she used to work."

"What do you mean 'where she used to work'?"

"My lord, that was some bang on the head. Surely you can't have forgotten Claire was murdered in 2017. Dierdre and Lucy too. Some psycho serial killer got life in a secure hospital."

I could not find any words. I felt confused. All I could think was Dave must have got his dates mixed up. Typical of him.

"Phil, you don't seem fussed."

"About what?"

"Chambers building and Claire's old office bombed, that's what. And, you see that guy over there?" Pointing to another man on the ward, he continued, "He got injured because of a third bomb in Holborn. Someone blew up the Insolvency Office."

I shrugged but said nothing.

"Tell me it wasn't you."

"It wasn't me. Happy?"

"It doesn't matter if I'm happy or not, I think the police will want to talk to you."

Turning away from me, Brad almost sprinted out of the ward. I looked across at the man in the bed. He too was sitting upright. *I know you,* I thought.

TWENTY-NINE

CHAPTER 28

The ward had quietened down with all visitors gone, the nurses had completed dispensing medications and were all assembled at the nurses' station for handover. It was safe to make my move. Throwing one leg out after the other, I tested my balance, still holding the side of the hospital bed. I felt okay. Moving slowly, I walked to the left side of the other man's bed to free up my good right arm. I was standing next to the cabinet with the patient resting on his left side and to my right. I heard him snoring lightly. Looking at the clipboard above his head, I read his name. Jeffrey... Jeffrey Vincent.

My mind was in turmoil. All I could hear was that damn voice in my head, *'the Official Receiver guy. The one who conned you at the interview.'* But that was Vincent, or Vincent's voice, who insisted I add him to the list. I have no clue as to what is happening.

A pair of scissors lay on top of the bedside cabinet, carelessly forgotten by a nurse. I scooped them up, holding them in my right hand. I prodded the snoring man who turned to face me, looking both annoyed and quizzical. "Do you recognise me?" I whispered.

"No."

"What's your name?"

"Why?"

"You sure you don't know me? I remember you well. You interviewed me after my bankruptcy at the Insolvency Office in Holborn. Stitched me up good and proper, you did. Now do you remember?"

"The barrister."

"Yes, but not for much longer thanks to you. I'm in court for perjury soon and no doubt you will be the star witness. What is your name?"

"Vincent."

He had just signed his death warrant. First, I plunged the scissor blades right into his chest, then his neck, and both eyes. He screamed but I continued in my stabbing frenzy until I heard a nurse scream and a voice somewhere in a hazy distance shouting, "Put the knife down, now!"

Too late, Vincent was dead.

The detectives, two of them, questioned me for five hours that night, and another six hours the following day. The questions initially were about the stabbing of Vincent. I learned he ended up in hospital when he caught the blast from the Insolvency Service explosion as he walked his dog along the street. He lived close to where he worked.

The detectives soon got tired of my constant "no comment' to every single question, even the innocuous ones like when I was asked for my name. But it was clear they had a watertight case against me and knew all about my bankruptcy and impending court appearance for perjury.

The questioning then went on to ask me what I knew about the three bombings. I once more exercised my right to silence. I learned more from them than they from me. Dave had been arrested. He spilled the beans completely, naming me as the prime mover in the plan. It didn't help Dave or me that he had been in possession of some of the C4 explosive, detonators, and mobile phones on his arrest. I also discovered why he had set off the bombs a day earlier than agreed. The thirty thousand was burning a hole in his pocket. He had bought a large consignment of drugs, including heroin, to set himself up as a dealer. The trouble was he went back to his old ways. He sampled too much product and in the words of the detective, Dave made a decision. "'Fuck it,' he said. 'I'll do it a day early. I can't do it when I'm off my head 'cos I'll likely blow myself up.' Once a smackhead, always a smackhead, eh, Mister Mercer?"

Once more, I said, "No comment," but couldn't resist a half smile as I should have known better.

My second day in the police station culminated with me being charged. One of murdering Jeffrey Vincent, and one of conspiracy to cause explosions. The perjury charge was discontinued owing to the vital evidence of Jeffrey Vincent no longer a viable option, though the Department of Business and Innovation, the prosecution agency, did consider having the statement admitted in evidence under the hearsay exception rule.

A long eighteen months followed. I was in custody, remanded to Her Majesty's Prison Woodthorpe, a high security prison in Bedfordshire. It contained a hospital wing for psychiatric patients. There, I was medicated with goodness know what, and regularly interviewed by two doctors, one a psychiatrist, the other a psychologist. I was also twice seen by Doctor Karl Nilsson, a preeminent psychiatrist and expert witness. He was also qualified in psychology as well as psychiatry.

My date for sentencing was eventually set for the Central Criminal Court, the Old Bailey. I had much earlier attended an arraignment when it was decided I wasn't fit to enter a plea owing to my mental illness. I had no doubt I would end up in an institution for the criminally insane. That was especially the case after I read Nilsson's expert report prepared for the sentencing hearing. I did not expect, nor had I reason to, everything that was contained in that report. Much of it came as a shock. That is putting it mildly. But it did explain things.

THIRTY

CHAPTER 29

John Kay, Queen's Counsel, visited me at Woodthorpe. I was surprised as I hadn't instructed a solicitor so how could a leading barrister represent me? He explained the Ministry of Defence had instructed him directly, bypassing the usual channels. That also surprised me.

I liked John Kay. He was a no-nonsense guy, originally from Liverpool but had lost his native twang apart from the odd flat vowels. I had never met him before, but he put me at ease despite the surroundings and the circumstances. It was through him I learned about what Nilsson was likely to say to the judge at sentencing. He also explained to me the hearing would be held *in camera*, an unusual thing but apparently the government at highest level had issued an embargo on all media reporting so the Old Bailey judge had no choice but to hold the hearing behind closed doors.

Two weeks after this visit, I was driven to London in a small prison van. We set off at eight that morning. It was ten when the van swung through the gates at the rear of the Old Bailey, a court I was truly familiar with. I also knew its long history, stretching back to its association with the mediaeval Newgate Gaol. Yet, I didn't feel like a prisoner on the way to the gallows. I almost felt relief. Closure is the modern word for how I was feeling.

The heavy steel-reinforced door leading to the cells opened after one of my guards pressed a bell. I was ushered first to a desk where I was searched and 'booked in,' then to a cell where I was the solitary inmate. The steel door clanged shut behind the guard, giving me time to look around. I knew this cell so well from my barrister days. It still bore the same graffiti on the walls ''Kilroy is innocent.' Ten minutes later, the wicket gate – the flap in the middle of the door, dropped, a small tray with a sandwich and coffee atop the tray. Gratefully, I said a 'thank you' to the unseen guard, took the tray inside the cell and flipped open the bread to check the contents. Sausages and HP sauce, nice, I thought. Five minutes after finishing the sandwich and coffee, John Kay came to see me in the cell.

"Phil, good morning."

"Good morning," I replied.

"We really have nothing to discuss as we went through it all at Woodthorpe prison, unless you want to talk over anything with me." I knew why he was saying that. One, he was right, and two, it saved him finding an empty interview room in the cell block.

"No, that's fine. I'll see you upstairs in court."

The guard let him out and closed the heavy gate, locking me in.

"The Crown and Philip Mercer," called the clerk. I was seated in the dock of Court Seven, one of the modernised courtrooms, unlike the museum-like courtrooms of Courts One and Two on the higher floors, famous for accommodating the trials of notorious killers in days of yore.

I could see the judge perched up above the clerk's desk. He was sitting directly below the coat of arms. I could also see John Kay, my counsel, together with counsel instructed by the Crown Prosecution Service. They were seated in the first long row below the clerk. The empty witness box was away to their right, close to the judge. Even if I swivelled my head, I knew I couldn't see the public gallery from my vantage point and anyway I knew it had been closed off.

"My Lord," Kenneth Watkins droned. He was prosecuting counsel and was now on his feet addressing the judge, who looked resplendent with the red sash across his ample chest. "I appear for the Crown and..."

His Honour Judge Harker interrupted him. "Mr Kay, what a delight to see you in my court. Mr Watkins, I am aware of the usual courtesies but there is no requirement to inform me who this is. Shall we proceed?"

"My Lord, as your Lordship wishes. As your Lordship is aware..."

"Mister Watkins. Please do not tell me of what I am aware. It is unknown matters I am interested in. Please make me aware of those." I had to stifle a snigger. This judge does not like Mr Watkins. "Mr Kay, are we ready to call some evidence?"

"My Lord, yes. Doctor Nilsson is here and ready. Detective Superintendent Evans will be here in about one hour, I am told by my learned friend, Mr Watkins."

He's got this judge eating out of his hand. That little introduction is usually the preserve of the Crown, not the defence. What's this Detective Superintendent all about?

"Very well, I suppose these are the court's witnesses, not the prosecution's? They are here to give evidence to assist me as to whether or not I impose a hospital restriction order on Mister Mercer."

"My Lord, that is correct," Watkins said, leaping to his feet, trying to save face.

The judge ignored him. "Call Doctor Karl Nilsson," he called to the court usher.

While the court waited for the doctor to arrive, the judge reminded all present, "This court is now *in camera*. Counsel, the prisoner in the dock, his guards with him in the dock, my clerk, and the ushers will remain. All others must leave this courtroom."

That decree applied to a handful of people sitting behind prosecution counsel. They were all Crown Prosecution Service employees with no role to play in the proceedings.

THIRTY-ONE

CHAPTER 30

"Doctor Nilsson. You have taken the oath. I will forgo the formality of you establishing your expertise. It is so well recognised I find it an otiose exercise. I have read with great interest your sixty-page findings. I will use that report as the basis for my final ruling. In the interim, please explain in lay terms various parts of your findings," Judge Harker said.

"My Lord, I will." The doctor was dressed exactly as he had on our two previous encounters. He wore a dark grey suit and a pale blue shirt with a vivid red necktie. He looked more like a business executive than one of the top experts in his field. Indeed, with his cropped blond hair, tanned face, and strong jaw, he looked more like a celebrity actor.

"Perhaps, first, you can tell us about your diagnosis?"

"My Lord, yes. Philip Mercer is suffering from Post-Traumatic Stress Disorder, commonly referred to as PTSD, a disorder of the mind as classified by the WHO."

"WHO?"

"World Health Organisation. It divides, let me use the term 'mental illness' for simplicity, mental illness into various coded classifications."

"Is his condition treatable?"

"Yes, if treated in the right conditions and over a long period of time."

"And those conditions are?"

"A closed community under psychiatric supervision."

"Making a hospital order essential? Is that correct, Doctor?"

"In my opinion, yes. There are also underlying issues closely associated with the diagnosis, making treatment more complex than it would be in normal circumstances."

"And those issues are?"

"They fall under the heading of 'Dissociative amnesia.' It is one of a group of conditions called dissociative disorders. Dissociative disorders are mental illnesses that involve disruptions or breakdowns of memory, consciousness, awareness, identity, and/or perception. When one or more of these functions is disrupted, symptoms can result. These symptoms can interfere with a person's general functioning, including social and work activities, and relationships."

"When or how does it occur, Doctor?"

"It occurs when a person blocks out certain information, usually associated with a stressful or traumatic event, leaving him or her unable to remember important personal information. With this disorder, the degree of memory loss goes beyond normal forgetfulness and includes gaps in memory for long periods of time or of memories involving the traumatic event."

"Is it different than what most lay people know as amnesia?"

"Dissociative amnesia is not the same as simple amnesia, which involves a loss of information from memory, usually as the result of disease or injury to the brain. With dissociative amnesia, the memories still exist but are deeply buried within the person's mind and cannot be recalled. However, the memories might resurface on their own or after being triggered by something in the person's surroundings."

So far, nothing I wasn't expecting. Broadmoor, here I come.

"And the causes of PTSD?"

"There can be many different causes, but the essential feature is an event so shocking that it triggers an extreme reaction in the patient."

"And what was the event in this instant case?"

"A unique and tragic event. It was only uncovered through use of a deep hypnosis technique conducted over many sessions with Mister Mercer. That and the use of powerful drugs."

"This discovery you mention. Is this why we are hearing evidence *in camera*?"

"Yes. As soon as I notified the Ministry of Defence, a D-Notice or gagging order was imposed save for judicial hearings such as this, meaning though the facts can be made known in this court today, the media cannot report those facts."

"Doctor Nilsson, I think it best if you now recount the patient's history for the record, which will remain sealed. After all, it's the patient's account that forms the basis of your conclusions, is that right?"

"Yes, indeed."

"One other thing before you start. Is there any possibility the patient, Mister Mercer, could be fabricating his account?"

"No, none at all. What he told us in those sessions is all demonstrably true."

"Perhaps this is a good time for you to recount what he told you before we hear the rest of your report?"

"Yes, my Lord."

THIRTY-TWO

CHAPTER 31

Extract from Doctor Nillson's Report

The following is how Philip Mercer recounted his experiences following the radical inhumane treatment he received:

Border Afghanistan and Pakistan 2002

By daylight, it was apparent we had a downhill trek in store. The overnight stop in the cave was the highest altitude point of our journey to god knows where. Following a breakfast of dry rations and water, Redbeard and Greybeard prodded us with their weapons and ordered us to move. The trail took us downwards all the way until we reached a fertile plain.

A highway of sorts stretched out as far as the horizon until I could make out another mountain range through the haze. Under our captor's direction, we walked towards the haze. Occasionally, the forced march halted to allow a vehicle to pass by. We were directed to either lie hidden in long grass or in an irrigation ditch running parallel with the road. The two Americans did the same. It was clear that whoever they were, discovery was to be avoided. This hiding routine became so frequent I started the practice of looking at Redbeard on hearing a vehicle's approach or as was more likely, on seeing trails of dust in the vehicle's wake. He would nod, then I would pull Tommy with me to hide. Our captors followed as usual.

Aside from some water to drink from their flasks, and that we had to drink without stopping, we received no nourishment. We trekked for hours even when the sun reached its zenith. At least now the pain in my jaw became secondary. The foot blisters and aching legs soon took over. Sideways glances at Tommy told me he was also exhausted.

As the sun dropped lower behind us, the mountain range I had seen earlier loomed larger. "Turn down this track," Redbeard commanded. There was a dirt track on our left, probably wide enough to accommodate a car or small truck. It was populated with small boulders and pot-holed in places. I was too weary to talk. Tommy too, I guess, as we didn't respond. We simply did as we were told.

About one hour later we approached a single-storey concrete building set back about two hundred yards in its own grounds. A razor wire topped fence ran all the way around its perimeter. Every hundred yards, a large pole stood proud of the fence and was crowned by a camera. As we walked up to the main gates, one of the cameras swung around in our direction. Seconds later, the gate opened.

In the building's reception area, I was amazed to see a sign written in three languages, including English. 'The Unit' part seemed a bit ominous. It seemed we were now in Pakistan. If I were a cat, I'd be curious – instead I was deeply worried. Just as well, seeing we know what happens to curious cats, nine lives or not. I wanted to live my life a lot longer. Redbeard instructed us to sit so he could remove the plastic cuffs. Greybeard kept guard while his colleague cut the plastic.

I was rubbing my wrist when I saw a tall burly guy with a pock-marked face join the four of us in the reception area. He was wearing a soldier's uniform decorated with braid on the epaulettes. I assumed he was an officer.

He spoke in an educated English manner. "First thing you need to know is there is no escape from the unit. Second thing is you will be freed if and when we deem it necessary. Thirdly, you will now be examined by a doctor. After that, you will be locked in your cells, fed and watered before the processing. Do you understand?"

"Yes, sir," I said deciding to play up to his obvious rank.

The two CIA guys slunk off somewhere. Tommy and I were separated.

After a while, I was taken to another room inside the building. There was a man inside the room dressed in a white doctor's house coat. He also wore wire-framed spectacles with round lenses, giving him a boffin-like aura. He stood about five feet-seven inches and as skinny as a rake. When he spoke, it was with an American accent, but I thought there was a German inflection. I immediately thought of the Nazi concentration camp doctors for some reason. "Lie down." He pointed to a gurney at the far side of the room. He ran his hands along my jaw for a minute or so.

'Hmm, I heard you had to be subdued. That mandible needs wiring.'

I assumed he was talking about my jaw. "I'd rather you didn't touch it," I said.

"Please yourself, you will probably end up with a lopsided jaw if it's not wired."

"I'll take my chances."

"You need to wait here. The armed guard will remain at the door."

"Wait? What for?"

"Another doctor. He will administer some injections."

"Why can't you do that?"

"Look, soldier, it's best you stop asking questions. Do you know what happens in the Unit?"

"I got the feeling this guy was okay and might help me. "No idea. What the hell are some Americans and Pakistanis doing kidnapping two British soldiers? Tell me that." I was hoping the CIA or whoever would interrogate us, but confident we would be released on confirming our identities.

"My friend. Clearly you know nothing of the tangled politics of the region. Nothing about the clandestine close cooperation between Pakistan's Inter-Services Intelligence, the ISI, and the CIA. The accepted history of Pakistani involvement in Afghanistan was that it supported the Afghan Mujahideen against the Soviet Union during the Soviet–Afghan War. Back then, the ISI worked in close coordination with the Agency to train and fund the Mujahideen with American, Pakistani, and Saudi funds.

"After the fall of the Soviet Union, the ISI provided strategic support and intelligence to the Afghan Taliban against America and its allies in the 1990s. That left some high-ranking ISI officers disgruntled. They no longer had access to CIA funds they had become accustomed to. No funds meant no siphoning of cash into private bank accounts unless these officers secretly collaborated with the CIA. That was why the 'Unit' was formed. It is operated jointly by the CIA and a rogue element of ISI."

"My mouth dried up. I croaked, "What does this Unit do?" I wasn't too sure I was going to like the answer.

"Its purpose is to conduct psychological experiments including brainwashing using torture, drugs, and hypnosis. They may spare you from the torture."

"This is outrageous, not to mention completely outside of the Geneva Convention."

"My friend, this is the CIA. Do you really think anyone will ever find out?"

"Why me? Why us?"

"I don't know. I'm just the physician. I make sure detainees aren't carrying some infectious disease."

"I don't get it. What's the point?"

"The point is, my friend, to prove their programming can make someone do something that would normally be an abomination. You have heard of the CIA's Project MK-Ultra experiments in the 1950s and '60s? Or Jacob's Ladder during the Vietnam war?"

"That was a book or movie. I saw the film. It's fiction."

"You think?"

The way he said it with not a glimmer of emotion made me shudder with fear. The doctor left the room. I wasn't sure whether to thank him or kill him. I felt helpless, powerless. The next white coat came into the room. I let him do what he needed to do. Three needles entered my arm, one following the other. The room spun and turned to a kaleidoscope of colours. The ceiling pressed into my face. I felt I was suffocating. I licked the ceiling. It tasted like vanilla ice cream. It was good. I could breathe. I had read enough about LSD to know I was experiencing an acid trip. It lasted for a whole day and I saw a whole new world of beauty with colours and patterns I had never been aware of previously. I also felt my ego, my very being, reduced in importance drastically. No longer was I the centre of the universe and that was when I experienced communing with God. I learned to be dependent on the people keeping me captive. That was the paradox – I no longer felt like a prisoner.

Days of sleep deprivation followed with no food. I had no contact with anyone. I was allowed some water but not much; a plastic water bottle was thrown into my cell through an open flap occasionally. I saw no one open or close the flap. I had not seen Tommy since we arrived at this hellhole. Then the injections continued. Every day, twice a day for I don't know how long. I lost track of time. I lost track of everything including my identity, location, what I did. Have you ever been there? Not knowing who you are? I was terrified. Yes, I did see people at this point. I saw the Pashtun guards and Americans. Not the two who took me prisoner. These two Americans seemed like doctors. Acted and talked like doctors, then wham! They would change into gangsters. Threatening me, slapping me. They waterboarded me too. Still I was kept starved, but the water rations increased.

Next stage was the hole. It was in the yard. It was about ten feet deep so no way of escape. It was full of shitty water. I mean literally shit. There were turds floating all around me. They weren't all mine. The water was about two feet in depth. I think a small-diameter sewer pipe fed into the hole. The rats were as big as cats. I knew they were trying to break me but as much as I tried to resist that, I knew I was getting weaker mentally and physically. If they'd given me a gun, I'd have topped myself. Little did I know there was worse to come.

I have no clue how long I was kept in that hole. I recall I woke up in a clean room. I have no idea how or when I was taken there. The room was white… everything was white. Even the camera housings containing the cameras were white metal. There was a bed in the room with white sheets and pillow cover. The room was about fifty to sixty feet square, white walls and a low white ceiling. The white ceiling fan was the only noise in there… for a while. I received food and plenty of water whilst I was in the white room. The lights were turned off at night and I slept well for the first time in weeks. It seemed like they were building up my physical strength. One of the doctors I had seen previously came in twice a day to administer injections. I had no clue why, but they made me feel disoriented.

After a few more days, the Pashtun guards wheeled in a TV set. It sat on top of a trolley. They would switch it on, only leaving when the picture flickered into life. It must have been a taped video feed because it showed the same thing continuously. At first, I was unable to make out the figure cowering in the corner of a dark room. Adjusting my eyes to the gloom, I came to realise it was Tommy. His beard was straggly, right down to his upper chest. It looked filthy. His head was shaven, probably to prevent infection from head lice but he had open sores all over his arms and legs.

I guess I had to endure watching Tommy in this video for about four weeks. It was every day for all that time. The same continuous loop over and over again until one day it became a live feed. Tommy was still in the same disgusting filthy state but now there were two men in the room besides Tommy. These two were dressed head to foot in baggy white suits with black cloth covering their heads. The cloth had eye slits but there was no way of identifying who these guys were. What followed was like a scene from the *Texas Saw Massacre* but worse. Using a chainsaw, they cut off one of Tommy's arms at the elbow. One of them went out of shot for a few seconds, returning with a blowlamp. He ignited it then cauterised the end of the stump. That was it… for now.

Some days later, the same two guys, or at least I thought they were as they were still covered in the same outfits, dragged Tommy into the room. I saw someone had bandaged his stump, you know, where they had amputated his arm. He was limp, wearing a dirty loincloth. I saw them smash his ankles with a sledgehammer. Both legs. Then they took the sledgehammer to both shins. I couldn't watch. He screamed. They shouted at him in English, "Shut up! Shut up!" They pushed him down on the dirty floor. He was now on his back. Punches rained in on his face and head until he went unconscious. One of the hooded guys pulled out a knife. The other pulled open Tommy's mouth. They cut out his tongue. The bastards.

The next day, I think, the live feed was put on again. He was leaping about on all fours like he was a dog, no doubt because he had lost the use of his legs. The soundtrack was awful. I heard him whimpering then barking just like a dog. I saw them train him to do that. They would do the barking noises and he would copy. As soon as he barked, they threw him raw meat. He ate that like a wild dog. They would laugh and look at the camera as if pointing at me. They would take it in turns shouting, "Look, Vincent! You will kill."

I didn't know it then, but this was all part of their brainwashing techniques.

It was the two white-coated doctors who indoctrinated me with the drugs and hypnosis sessions. I resisted to a point until my will was broken. It was they who first gave Tommy the name of 'Vincent.' Despite what they did to me I kept repeating, "I can't do it. That's Tommy. He's like a brother to me."

The doctors would constantly tell me, "That is not Tommy. It is Vincent. Look, he is inhuman. It's a dog, a mad dog. You MUST KILL IT."

I think it took about twelve weeks of drugs, hypnosis, and indoctrination to break me. I knew I had to kill Vincent, but I didn't know how or when.

They filmed it. I was taken to a courtyard outside the Unit building where I was handed a sword with a long-curved blade. I knew it was called a pulwar in Afghanistan. Vincent was locked in a small cage, howling like a dog. The guards released a door on the cage, so Vincent was released into the yard. It just stayed put in one place on all fours, panting. I heard a command, 'KILL IT.' I walked over to its head, took aim, and cut off its head with the pulwar. I beheaded Vincent.

A further long period of brainwashing took place. I can't say how long. I now know it erased all of this from my memory. When I say 'all,' I mean my deployment to Afghanistan, the capture, the Unit, and what happened there. All I recall is a flight back to England where I was hospitalised in an

Army hospital. You say your final report will deal with that.

THIRTY-THREE

CHAPTER 32

"What did happen on his return to England, Doctor Nilsson?" the Judge asked.

"Mister Mercer was firstly admitted to a MDHU..."

"I am aware we are *in camera* but no jargon or acronyms, please."

"Of course. He was first admitted to a Ministry of Defence Hospital Unit in Surrey. Once it became clear he was suffering from trauma, he was transferred to a special ward at another MDHU." The doctor continued without seeing the judge frowning or hearing him tap his pen. "It was there under close psychiatric care it was discovered what he had experienced in Afghanistan and later in Pakistan."

"I thought, for want of a better expression, his memory had been wiped clean."

"It had, but the team explored his subconscious using the same methods: drugs and deep hypnosis under carefully controlled conditions."

"I see."

"Painstakingly, they worked their way through all his experiences, ensuring he was returned to normality safely. These experiences were so traumatic it was properly decided to return him to a state of erased memory. In other words, to go back to where he was on arriving in England. One of the knock-on effects of that was he had no memory whatsoever of his deployment to Afghanistan or what happened subsequently. His memories of foreign language training with the Intelligence Corps were also erased."

"Was his wife aware of any of this?"

"My Lord, the short answer is 'yes.' There was a need to brief her owing to the fact he could no longer recall intimate moments between them such as where they first met. She was also a serving soldier in the Intelligence Corps, an officer. I understand Detective Superintendent Evans is to give evidence about Mrs Mercer."

"That is correct, Doctor. We will resume hearing your conclusions and recommendations after we hear from Mister Evans."

THIRTY-FOUR

CHAPTER 33

"I am Michael Evans, a Detective Superintendent in charge of the Metropolitan Police Service Special Branch."

"Mister Evans, all the parties have accepted your witness statement as your evidence-in-chief. It is not challenged. This hearing is *in camera* as you have no doubt noticed. Will you confirm it was you who organised the D-Notice issued by the Ministry of Defence?"

"My Lord, it was owing to the sensitive material that was bound to be disclosed in a normal court hearing."

"Thank you, will you now please tell us what your involvement was in this case and the result of your investigations?"

"In summary, Mrs Elizabeth Mercer, known as Liz, was briefed by the MOD..."

"MOD?" No one had warned Evans about this judge's dislike of acronyms.

Looking perplexed, Evans said, "Ministry of Defence, my Lord."

"Continue."

"After her husband, Mister Mercer here, returned to England and after it was realised he had a psychiatric problem. The reason for that was because the authorities feared he could relapse if certain triggers came into play. Those triggers would include..."

"Mister Evans, we have an expert psychiatrist here. Please leave the medical material to him."

"Yes, my Lord. There did come a time when Mrs Mercer suspected her husband was in danger of relapse owing to stress."

"Very well, we will hear about that later from the doctor. What did Mrs Mercer do following these suspicions?"

"She arranged to meet a Mister Joe Zaleh, an investigative journalist with the Guardian. She intended to act as a whistle-blower."

"Did she in fact meet him?"

"No, she was killed before they met."

"And Mister Zaleh?"

"Also killed, murdered, as was Liz Mercer."

"How were they killed?"

"Both injected with a nerve agent that closely mimics cancer."

"You know this, how?"

"Both bodies were exhumed after Mister Mercer's history came to light. The pathology reports confirmed the presence of the nerve agent in both deceased."

"Any suspects?"

"Yes, my Lord. I have been in close contact with the FBI... the Federal Bureau of Investigation, and through them, the CIA at Langley, Virginia. The... Central Intelligence Agency has cooperated to the extent of sending me a video taken at what was known as the Unit in Pakistan."

"Was?"

"It no longer exists. It was run by a rogue section. The two agents who ran it are believed to be in hiding in Bolivia."

"Do you have the video with you?"

"Yes."

"Before I do anything more, do counsel have anything to say about my proposal to view this video? May I add that Mister Mercer, his guards, and my court staff will be excluded from the courtroom during the playback. Doctor Nilsson. You may leave or stay."

Breaking with all legal conventions about who is permitted to address the court, the doctor said, "I will stay."

Both counsel got to their feet to say the same thing: "Nothing to add, my Lord."

"Mr Watkins, would you like to operate the playback machine, seeing it is in front of you?"

"My Lord, yes," said counsel for the prosecution.

It was twenty minutes later my guards and I were summoned back to the courtroom. I don't know if it was my imagination, but I detected a sympathetic look from the judge.

"Returning to Mrs Mercer, Superintendent, was there any record of communications between her and the Guardian newspaper?"

"Indeed, my Lord. I was able to retrieve an email sent by Liz Mercer to Mr Zaleh through my inquiries with GCHQ at Cheltenham. I have a copy of it with me. My inquiry with

GCHQ also revealed a type of journal kept by Mrs Mercer."

"What form did this journal take?"

"It was an electronic diary written in a Word document. Staff at GCHQ were able to retrieve it from the Microsoft servers."

"Very well, please read aloud both the email and the contents of the journal."

I saw the detective holding a piece of A4 paper. After putting his glasses on, he read out the contents of the email.

"From liz.mercer@tmail.co.uk to joe.zaleh@theguardian.co.uk dated the 25th April, 2017. Dear Mr Zaleh, I do hope you take this email seriously and eventually we meet. In the meantime, here's what you need to know. My husband, Philip Mercer, was deployed to Afghanistan in 2002. He was a Sergeant with the Intelligence Corps embedded with Marines and a small attachment of 2 Para. To cut a long story short, he and a colleague were taken prisoner. It turned out they were captured by rogue elements of the CIA, and taken to Pakistan forcibly where they were tortured, and in my husband's case brainwashed. He was forced to kill his colleague, Lance Corporal Tommy Owens also of the Intelligence Corps. Tommy was his best man at our wedding. This was part of a CIA experiment with brainwashing using deep hypnosis and the use of drugs.

"I was also Intelligence Corps but was never deployed outside the UK. When my husband eventually returned to England he was hospitalised, diagnosed with PTSD and Dissociative Identity Disorder. The doctors decided to perform a reverse brainwashing procedure to erase all memory of Afghanistan and what happened there. This had already been done by the rogue unit but had to be performed again to ensure its success. It worked, but it also erased his memories of our wedding and Tommy. I was briefed on all this and with my blessing a story was concocted to prevent Phil from ever discovering the truth.

"This involved doctoring all our wedding photographs to remove Tommy from them and inventing a story as to how he got his jaw broken. He, Phil, believed he did it playing rugby when in reality it happened after he was captured in Afghanistan. His army records were also altered to hide any deployment in Afghanistan. In short, he was reverse brainwashed by the MOD so he suffered a form of amnesia about his awful experience.

"His brother was also told as they were close. In fact, Barry, his brother almost gave the game away in a phone chat with Phil. Barry mentioned Afghanistan but changed tack rapidly when he realised his gaffe. Barry recently died and I have suspicions about that. I believe it may be connected to Phil and Afghanistan in some way.

"The reason I have contacted you is because I strongly believe my husband is suffering symptoms of some kind of serious breakdown. He's having night terror attacks, keeps shouting the name 'Vincent,' and 'kill it, kill all of them.'

I'm scared he is going to do something terrible. I approach you owing to your track record of dealing with state secrets involving whistle-blowers. I'm desperate for some help and I don't know who to turn to as I certainly don't trust the government. Can we please meet as a matter of urgency? Yours, Liz Mercer."

"Mister Mercer, would you like a short break? I can see you are affected by that testimony, and understandably so."

"Please carry, on. I'm okay," I said but I didn't feel okay at all. *This was the first time I knew any of this. Poor Liz!*

"Very well, carry on, Mr Evans," the judge said.

Detective Superintendent Evans commenced reading Liz's journal.

THIRTY-FIVE

CHAPTER 34

I'm writing this journal to record certain events and my thoughts in connection with what happened to my husband, Philip Mercer. I write in the hope that if anything happens to me or my husband, this journal will help bring those responsible to justice. I have good reason to fear something bad is going to happen to Phil, me, and possibly his brother. Recently, I was followed around my local supermarket by a stranger. I thought I had shaken him off but on reaching the checkout, I saw him behind me. It was then I felt a sharp pain in the back of my leg like a wasp had stung me. On turning around, the man had gone. Now, a few weeks later, I feel sick. I have no appetite or sense of smell. I'm just pecking at food but my taste buds aren't the same and I have a metallic taste in my mouth. I am worried and have made a doctor's appointment for next week.

The real worrying thing is Barry, Phil's brother, told me on the phone he was experiencing strange symptoms after some random guy bumped into him at the petrol station where he lives in Australia. That was while he was waiting to pay for his petrol. The thing with Barry and I started after I contacted a Guardian journalist. I emailed him to arrange to meet so I could tell him all about what happened to Phil in Afghanistan. Now, I found out the journalist is dead. Someone or some organisation, even a government is trying to keep these things hidden. This all started in 2003.

The phone call I took at our married quarters, our home, was cryptic. All the caller said was, "Captain Mercer, pack a bag. Civvies, no uniform. You're going to Islamabad. A car will be outside your door at exactly 1400 hours." I knew then it was something to do with Phil.

The next day, I arrived at the British High Commission in Islamabad where I was greeted by an attaché who I suspect was MI6. "Captain... Mrs Mercer, this is delicate. We, or rather security, found a man opposite our building yesterday. He was in a distressed condition and we came to believe he may be British; that was confirmed when his fingerprints were identified as a serving soldier reported MIA in Afghanistan. We believe he's your husband, Mrs Mercer."

I said something like, "Oh, my God! Let me see him."

The man in the suit showed me through to a room with a bed in it. It was like a first aid room. I saw Phil sitting in a chair. He stared at me for about thirty seconds until he started to cry. They were uncontrollable tears. I put my arms around him to comfort him. He stood to hold me close. That was when I could feel he'd lost weight. We held each other for five minutes. He cried all that time until I said, "Phil, it's okay. We can go home soon."

"Liz? Is this really you?" he said. He was dazed and confused.

It was obvious to me there was something seriously wrong with him. The next day we were flown back to Britain and I went with Phil to a Military Hospital Unit. He was then transferred to another unit specialising in psychiatry. It was part of the complex at Porton Down, the chemical warfare place. It became clear he was suffering from a form of PTSD brought on by the trauma of what had happened to him and Tommy Owens in that CIA camp. His memory of what happened there had been wiped clean. He knew me and knew he was in the Intelligence Corps, but they had erased all memories of Afghanistan, his capture with Tommy, and the truth of what happened in the Unit. Through a kind of reversal procedure, I was told they had managed to have Phil relive all that happened. After that discovery, they in effect brainwashed him again. That took a long time.

In effect, they engineered his brain to accept an alternative version of his life and history. The alternative version kept much in place. He was still married to me and had an army record in first the military police then the Intelligence Corps. That's where I first met him. All mention of service in Afghanistan was expunged. His medical records were altered to explain his broken jaw, attributing it to a rugby injury instead of the truth.

As part of this process the MOD briefed me and his brother, Barry, because they were close. I was told that his reverse brainwashing was a complete success but warned to look out for future symptoms. These symptoms could include nightmares, feelings of paranoia or hearing voices. They further explained that stress could induce symptoms. That's what happened. First, he had problems with his income tax. He refused to discuss that with me. Then came the night terror attacks with him shouting "Vincent" in his sleep. He also shouted, "Kill him," and "Kill it." I also found him burning stuff in our backyard. When I asked him about it, he got angry and we fought. It was obvious to me there was something wrong. I was worried sick.

I feel compelled to write about it because Phil is a decent, caring man, and a loving husband. The events in Afghanistan changed his life. He was experimented on and that's not right. I want someone to answer for all they did, the terrible things they did out there.

THIRTY-SIX

CHAPTER 35

Having read out Liz's journal entry and the email, the Special Branch detective stepped down from the witness box. He was now sitting in the row behind prosecution counsel. Doctor Nilsson was standing there ready to continue his evidence. Waiting for me and the guards to settle, the judge resumed, "Doctor Nilsson. I remind you, you are still sworn, under oath."

"Yes."

"Good, let us continue. What is your recommendation as to disposal of this case? A hospital order is clearly appropriate but with or without restriction?"

"With restriction, my Lord, is my professional opinion. It is essential that Mister Mercer is kept in hospital for as long as necessary, so he continues to receive the necessary therapeutic treatment in a secure environment."

"Very well. Mr Watkins, what happened to David Walton, the other man named on the conspiracy indictment?"

"My Lord, on the twenty-eighth December 2020, he was sentenced to twelve years imprisonment on the single count of conspiracy to cause explosions following a plea of guilty."

"Philip Mercer, please stand."

I stood and I knew what was coming.

"It falls to me to sentence you today. At an earlier time and before me in this court, you entered a plea of not guilty to murder relying on a defence of automatism, later judged to be insane automatism and so resulted in the special verdict of 'not guilty by reason of insanity' rather than simple acquittal. To put that in simpler words, it was found you had no control over your actions when you killed Mr Vincent through no fault of our own. You had been reprogrammed by rogue elements of a foreign agency and much of your memory wiped clean.

"It now falls to me, having heard medical evidence on the matter and with regard to two expert reports including that of Dr. Nilsson, to make an order in this sad and unusual case. Indeed, this is as tragic a case as I have encountered in my experience at the Bar and on the Bench. Nevertheless, my duty compels me to make a hospital order with restriction. I am sure Mr Kay, your eminent counsel, will explain all the ramifications to you. Take him down."

I was already spinning around on my heels as I heard the judge's last three words. I wasn't upset or annoyed. I knew what to expect.

Perhaps the treatment will work even if it takes many years. I hope so.

THIRTY-SEVEN

CHAPTER 36

Fifteen Years Later

Hunching down into my second favourite navy-blue, woollen overcoat didn't help. I'd almost forgotten what my first favourite felt like. I had been here in Broadmoor, a high security psychiatric hospital, for the past fifteen years. Despite the warm coat, I could still feel the biting easterly cut right through me, and the bright sunshine was deceptive. I shuddered, thinking of the warm room I had left behind. Still, at least I was now allowed to work outside in the vegetable garden. Digging the cold earth brought forth the pungent smell of brown fertile soil. Occasionally, the blade of the spade would strike flint in the shape of small rocks. It made the sparks fly, reminding me of sparklers on Bonfire Night as a kid. I was alone with my thoughts on a bitterly cold November day... *in a nut house of all places*. The politically correct don't like that phrase but if you were incarcerated here for years, you'd understand. *How else would you describe the likes of Peter Sutcliffe, the Yorkshire Ripper? He is a nut.* There were no longer noises or voices in my head. Life was good given the circumstances and maybe I'll get a discharge back into the community in the next couple of years.

There was a routine I stuck to digging the vegetable patch. Not so much a patch because it must have been about two-hundred square metres of land. It butted up to a high wall topped with razor wire on the eastern side of the complex. In the mornings I would dig up the fresh root vegetables, placing them in a wheelbarrow to later take to the kitchen. The afternoons were spent digging up the land that had lain fallow, breaking up the soil and making a pile of weeds for composting.

If I hadn't struck a small rock, I would never have seen him. The sparks flew off the blade as always. I paused to take a little breather and that was when I saw him. He was stealing vegetables from the wheelbarrow. I'd never seen him before but knew he wasn't staff owing to his demeanour. The staff had this air about them. An air of confidence that at some point that day, they would go home.

I wasn't that bothered about him stealing. I wasn't angry. In fact, when I walked up to him, I calmly said, "Who are you? I've not seen you around before."

"Charlie, Charlie Atkins," he said looking serious. "I was going to grab some for a hooch I'm making. You know, some poteen. Is that okay?"

"Yeah, sure, just ask next time." I could see him studying my face.

"Do I know you?" he said.

"No idea, do you?"

"Wait. I got it. You were the fucker who killed those women in the disused airfield."

"What are you talking about?"

"I saw you. The police charged me and here I am, all because of you."

Atkins punched me in the face.

Months later, during therapy sessions, I discovered I had battered him to the ground with my spade and then decapitated him using the spade's sharp blade. I don't remember any of it.

Essex police got a warrant to transfer me to Harlow Police Station for questioning. It didn't worry me. I enjoyed the trip out.

Two detectives entered the bare room. The younger one switched on a tape machine. The elder of the two did the talking.

"Mister Mercer, I must remind you this interview is being tape recorded. Present in the room are myself, Detective Superintendent Dick Jewell, and Detective Sergeant Michele Kapugi from the Essex Police Cold Cases Unit, your solicitor Mrs Smith, and the appropriate adult Mrs Khan.

"I will now read you your rights. You have been arrested on suspicion of the murders of Claire Munro, Dierdre Summers, and Lucy Fairweather in 2017. You do not have to say anything, but it may harm your defence if you do not mention when questioned something which you later may rely on in court. Anything you do say may be given in evidence. Do you understand?"

"I do."

"For the sake of the tape, please state your name."

"Philip Mercer."

"Thank you."

"Superintendent, please take note that Mister Mercer will answer 'no comment' to all questions as is his legal right," Mrs Smith said.

"Noted, but that does not prevent me from asking questions," Jewell said.

"Did you own a car in 2017?"

"No comment."

"A black Volvo V90 estate, registration YX 329 XZY to be exact?"

"No comment."

"You gave this car to Kasia Nowak, your former house help, following your arrest for the murder of Jeffrey Vincent, isn't that right?"

"No comment."

"Not to worry. You must know we can prove that if we need to.

"As I said, I'm from the Cold Cases Unit so please allow me to tell you what we discovered as a result of new advanced DNA testing procedures. The clothing of all three victims, Claire, Dierdre, and Lucy was tested for fibres. Guess what? Identical fibres were found on the outer clothing of all three women. Further analysis revealed they all originated from the soundproofing material in one specific make of car.

"That car was the Volvo V90. Okay, there are thousands of that make and model in Britain, but we ran a check on those seen on the ANPR cameras, automatic number plate recognition, on the M11 Motorway in 2017. Yes, we do keep that database so long, Mister Mercer. Your car was seen six times in the week these women were killed."

"Stop there. I need to speak with my solicitor in private," I said.

Switching off the tape, the detectives left us alone in the interview room but before I spoke to my solicitor, I insisted the appropriate adult leave too. She did.

"What disclosure did they provide to you before this interview started?"

"I was starting to tell you, but you were adamant you had nothing to answer for in relation to these allegations."

"I had nothing to do with those deaths but now I need to know what they know."

"You already know they can tie in your old car to the location and the fibres tie in your car, specifically the boot of your car, to the clothing of all three women. But more importantly, the police recovered a button from Lucy's coat. They found it in your car boot when they seized the car from Kasia as evidence. It has your DNA on it.

"The Crown will say the button snapped off when she struggled with you as you put her in the boot, and it lay there undiscovered for all these years. The prosecution case is based on that evidence. They will say you abducted all three and tied them up in the boot of your car before you took them to the disused airfield."

"What about Atkins?"

"It's obvious what they will say about him. He lived as a tramp, a homeless loser with psychiatric issues, in the abandoned building, who possibly saw you kill the women. He had intercourse with the last victim but that was the extent of his criminality. That explanation may convince a jury at your trial and explain away the DNA evidence that tied in Atkins to the killings."

"Hmm."

"I need to know your instructions."

"My instructions are let them prove it. We go back in and tell them I'm not saying another word. The interview is terminated."

"You're sure? Final?"

"Final."

THIRTY-EIGHT

CHAPTER 37

Crown Prosecution Service Case Conference, Harlow, Essex

"This is like déjà vu. Once more we are discussing the killings of those three women after all this time. I expressed my misgivings about the evidence in respect of Charlie Atkins. I was a DI then and your predecessor said it was all a matter for the jury as there was a realistic prospect of conviction. She was right. He was convicted, an innocent man, and this bastard Mercer did all three of them," Detective Superintendent Jewell said.

"And he murdered Atkins, sir," DS Kapugi added.

"My bet is Atkins confronted him in Broadmoor after recognising him. Told him what he'd seen, and they were Charlie Atkins' final words," Jewell said.

"That's probably correct, Mister Jewell, but we can't get that into evidence, can we?" Ms Sarah Stanning, Senior Crown Prosecutor said.

"True, but the scientific evidence is strong against Mercer so why the recommendation that there is no prosecution?"

"It passes the evidential test but it's not in the public interest to put him on trial."

"Why? Just because he's already serving on a restricted hospital order as the shrinks say he has PTSD and can't recall fuck all?"

"In a nutshell, yes. But it's more complicated than that. The defence can't use what caused the PTSD in open court. Anyway, what's the point? He's already restricted and in a secure psychiatric hospital, probably for the rest of his life."

"Sometimes the criminal justice system stinks."

"Yes, it does," said Ms Stanning.

THIRTY-NINE

CHAPTER 38

My transfer to Her Majesty's Prison Wakefield happened five weeks after I received the letter from The CPS informing me they would not be charging me with the murders of Claire Munro, Dierdre Summers, and Lucy Fairweather. It probably wasn't a coincidence. The medical team at Broadmoor seemed to have given up on me. Their collective medical opinion was I was now untreatable. It followed, according to their reasoning, I was now fit enough to join the general population, albeit on the lifers' wing at a high security prison.

There's nothing I can do or say that's going to change that. I can't say I'm delighted because Broadmoor had become my home. I knew it and it knew me. I will miss the vegetable patch. I know Wakefield will be high walls topped with razor wire, drab blocks of stone buildings with echoing corridors, standard cells and regimentation. I've heard some of the screws are nasty pieces of work. I suppose one of the differences now is having to face a parole hearing instead of a mental health tribunal. I try not to think about release though as it's unlikely to happen. I mean... would you release me? You would never know what triggers may make me kill again. I don't know what they are so how would anyone else know? All I do know is stress factors trigger the need to kill, then I have no recollection at all of the killings.

How else do I explain the dream of killing Claire, Dierdre, and Lucy when they were already dead? And I didn't kill Piers or Brad except in my dream. Perhaps one day, the truth will out about what happened in Afghanistan, and conceivably people will understand. For now, and as long as I breathe, I manage my life from day to day in confinement. Isn't that punishment enough?

Three Weeks Later HMP Wakefield

I'd just started to settle into my new routine. The food is pretty good and the screws aren't as bad as rumour had it. The library was good too and I had my own laptop in my cell which I use to start writing my life story, though it's odds on it will never be published owing to the Afghanistan thing. I mean, if the court was subject to a gagging order, then I'm pretty sure my story will never see daylight.

Frank Towell got friendly with me. He was another inmate serving a life sentence. Someone must have told him about me as he asked lots of questions about the criminal law. It got to a point where I was holding a law clinic in the library twice a week. They had an outdated copy of Archbold, the criminal practitioner's 'bible.' Most of the inmates pronounced it as Archybold. Though most questions were inane, I humoured them as it was a good way of making friends and in jail that's one of the keys to survival and sanity.

Often when the other lifers had gone, Frank would ask me questions about my conviction and surprisingly the murders of the three women. This made me suspicious as I was aware a well-known police tactic was to use 'cell confessions,' real or fabricated, as part of a prosecution case.

One day about ten weeks into my stint at Wakefield, one of the friendlier screws told me Frank had been transferred. I thought nothing of it until I was told to go to an interview room. Once I walked in, I was surprised to see Detective Superintendent Jewell once more. Detective Sergeant Kapugi was also there together with my solicitor.

Once Jewell had wrapped up the usual formalities, he placed a tape into a second tape player. The first machine was recording the interview with me. I listened closely to every word Frank said on that tape. You guessed, he made out I confessed to killing all three women. Not content with that, he also said I'd killed Charlie Atkins because not only had he recognised me, but I had recognised him. It was all bullshit, of course.

The police had already done all their homework before interviewing me and also held a case conference with the CPS prior to the interview. So, when I answered 'no comment' to all questions, yet again, Detective Superintendent Jewell formally charged me with the murders of Claire Munro, Dierdre Summers, and Lucy Fairweather.

Now, I wait for the trial date.

FORTY

CHAPTER 39

The trial was moved from Essex to Leeds on security grounds as it was closer to Wakefield, but the only problem for me was that I spent the nights in HMP Leeds, a shithole compared to Wakefield.

On the first day of trial and after I had pleaded not guilty to all three counts of murder at arraignment, counsel Elaine Weeldon made an application to stay proceedings on my behalf. She argued that it was impossible for me to have a fair trial as the defence was prohibited from adducing any evidence connected to Afghanistan. The court went behind closed doors to hear the legal argument. She also argued it was relevant as it cast considerable doubt on Towell's deposition. It wasn't until the following day the trial judge ruled in my favour. That was the end of that. Miss Weeldon told me in the cells after the ruling she was certain the government had intervened to ensure none of that Afghanistan evidence ever entered the public domain.

The big downside of the aftermath was I was kept locked up at HMP Leeds. It must be the worst prison in the country. The staff are demoralised and don't give a damn about anything owing to the cramped and decrepit building. Smuggling of contraband is rampant. If you want something, it can be got whether drugs, mobile phones or just about anything at all.

There were just two classes of inmates; those on remand waiting trial and convicted persons in general population. As a lifer, I wasn't in any special wing. I got banged up with a Londoner called Mikey. Still, no call to complain as we were the only two in the cell – some cells accommodated three prisoners in a small space.

Mikey seemed okay. We would sit together in the canteen at mealtimes. He was serving a seven year stretch for drug dealing, he told me. We were chatting away at lunch when the lights went out – literally for me. Suddenly his mood changed. He growled at me, "You don't have a clue who I am, do you?"

"No, should I?"

"I'm Ben Turner's son."

"Who?"

"My dad used to shack up with Claire Munro. He still had a thing for her after they split up."

"Right, I remember now."

"Funny how your memory is okay when it suits you."

I was about to reply when I saw him whip the top off a small bottle. He threw the clear liquid at my face. I heard the screws shouting and screaming at Mikey while some others took me to the hospital wing to be treated. There was a limit to what they could do so under guard I was transferred to Leeds Infirmary. The surgeons performed skin grafts to the acid burns but there was nothing they could do about my eyesight.

I stayed in the Infirmary for three weeks and then it was time to remove the facial bandages. I heard one of the doctors say, "How does that feel, Mister Mercer?"

"I don't feel a thing and I can't see anything except darkness. The last time I recall being unable to see was years and years ago in

Afghanistan. I had been captured and blindfolded. That cowardly so-called mate of mine, Tommy Owens, threw his weapon down to save his own skin. If he had done what he was supposed to, we would never have been captured by those rogue CIA spooks."

As soon as I told them about Tommy being a coward, I wanted to suck those words right back inside me. Believe me, I had never mentioned that to anyone, alive or dead. I knew every word of everything I told the shrinks.

I am asking you to believe me. After all, what is truth? Some say truth is a commodity. Politicians, for example, treat it so. It was a politician who coined the expression, "economical with the truth," when he eventually confessed after he was literally caught with his pants down. In my case, and for most of the time, I was not aware of the truth. Now in hindsight, I know the terrible things I did. I ask you to accept it was not the "real me" who did evil, but it arose owing to my 'conditioning' at the hands of barbarians so many years ago.

My life now is a different one entirely from that in my Army days before Afghanistan. For one, I am permanently blind. I cannot see or read. All I have now is darkness and my thoughts racing through my mind.

Whether through the hallucinogenic powers of LSD or not, I did commune with God in Afghanistan. I still do in the darkness. He and I know the world has many secrets. States have secrets as do many people. Some of those secrets have been revealed to me and if you come closer, I'll whisper in your ear and reveal them.

"The heads of all governments, except China, are aliens. If you don't believe me, just look at them on television with no sound. That's how you know. The Chinese are an enlightened, ancient civilisation. They know how to prevent their leaders succumbing to the alien invaders. That's it, do with it what you think fit."

FORTY-ONE

EPILOGUE

Years Later - Ministry of Defence, Whitehall, London

"Sir, may I remind you about a decision regarding that Freedom of Information Act request... the one about Philip Mercer," asked Caroline Smyth, the minister's Permanent Under Secretary.

"Of course. Tell the inquirer no such records exist or have ever existed."

"Isn't it better to issue the usual 'neither confirm nor deny' statement?"

"Caroline, have you suddenly gone deaf? They – DO – NOT - EXIST."

"But, sir..."

"No buts about it, Caroline. Have you any idea the stink it would cause, not to mention the embarrassment to this government and that of the United States? It's best buried forever. It's history."

"I can understand all of that but what about ensuring nothing like it happens again in the future?" Caroline said.

"It was a time of war in Afghanistan. Bad things happen in war. That is never going to change."

"I feel sorry for Mercer. He did wrong, yes, but there were reasons behind it that he had no control over."

"He's been dead for years. He died in a secure mental hospital. So, what's the point? Besides the PM says no disclosure of any of the Mercer files. Are the PM's wishes and mine not sufficient reason for you?"

"Of course, I'll do as you ask."

"Good. Now forget the whole thing. It's in the best interests of all concerned, you must accept that. Sometimes the truth cannot be shared. Now, bring me that latest intelligence file on China, please."

THE END

FORTY-TWO

ACKNOWLEDGEMENTS

This was a story that kept coming to me and begged to be written. As many of you will know, it's not quite my usual style of work. This was no fast-paced thriller like many of my works of fiction. Nevertheless, it had to be told and was at times quite a challenge for several reasons, the least of which was it was outside my usual *comfort zone* – see what I just did?

At one time I got bogged down but then a wonderful new beta reader (new to me), Michele Kapugi, inspired me to write the story in the way you have just read. Possibly she thought that her inspiring words and thoughts were going to end up differently than it did. If so, I ask for her forgiveness and I hope she enjoys the result of her input that motivated me. In the event she refuses to forgive me, I hope that by naming a character after her will ensure she long remains one of my trusted team of beta readers.

I also acknowledge and give thanks to the other beta readers in my VIP group team including Tina Gonsales-Cavalier, Julie-Anne Dalchow, Sara Jo Montgomery, Connie Charron, and John Davies. Thanks also to all the other fans and supporters in my VIP Facebook group. You all rock! I also thank Kay Castaneda, a fellow writer and member of my VIP group, for her words of encouragement on reading an excerpt of an early version of this book. I do value the feedback from all in the group.

I also thank Sheryl Lee once more for her editing skills including some excellent tips on developing this story.

Finally, the issue of mental health runs right through this book. I have strived to treat the subject with the utmost respect. I am no stranger to those serious issues in my own life, as any reader of my bestselling undercover cop memoir will know. Any form of mental health problem is serious and thank goodness we no longer live in an era when depression was scoffed at and admonished with a "pull yourself together."

I also suppose the issues of choice and the debate about nature versus nurture also run through this tale of suspense. Belay that – there is no "suppose" about it – they do. I mention that because a writer once said to me, a man with a similar legal background as mine, that people who do criminal acts have 'choices.' I strongly disagree if that person is suffering from a genuine mental illness.

Take Phil Mercer, for example, what dark secret from his past changes a decent man, and respected professional into a man with murder on his mind? Now you know.

If you enjoyed my efforts at keeping you entertained, please consider <u>*leaving a review of this book at the digital bookstore where you purchased it.*</u> *Only a few words are required, and those reviews are so important to authors like me. Thank you!*

ABOUT THE AUTHOR

Stephen Bentley is a former UK police Detective Sergeant, pioneering undercover cop, and barrister (criminal trial attorney). He is now a freelance writer and an occasional contributor to Huffington Post UK on undercover policing, and mental health issues.

His bestselling memoir, 'Undercover: Operation Julie - The Inside Story,' is a frank and fascinating insight into his undercover detective experiences during Operation Julie - an elite group of detectives who successfully investigated one of the world's largest drug rings. It has now been adapted for a feature film.

Stephen also writes crime fiction in a fast-paced plot-driven style including the *Steve Regan Undercover Cop Thriller* and the *Detective Matt Deal Thriller* series.

One of his short stories, 'The Rose Slayer,' won the SIA murder mystery competition in 2018, and has now been published in a multi-author anthology of murder mystery short stories, titled 'Death Among Us.'

His fiction draws heavily on his law enforcement background adding that ingredient of authenticity about which the legendary Raymond Chandler opined, "Fiction in any form has always intended to be realistic," when writing about "the detective story" in his essay 'The Simple Art of Murder'(1950). Stephen subscribes to that school of thought.

When he isn't writing, Stephen relaxes on the beaches of the Philippines with his family where he now lives, often with a cold beer and a book to hand.

You may find him on Twitter as @StephenBentley8 or connect with him at www.stephenbentley.info to signup to his mailing list.

LATEST RELEASE

Mercy: A Detective Matt Deal Thriller

Early Praise

"Hang on to your hat...this thriller is not for the faint-hearted!"

"Mercy is an awesome book ... It is a must read for anyone who loves a good thriller."

"The opening scene is gruesome and very descriptive but relevant to the whole story and its character building and the very purpose of Matt Deal and his justice that he needs to serve! ...Great book written well. Intense and an emotional rollercoaster. Big fat 5 stars!"

"Set in the future in post-Brexit U.K., the well-developed characters, plot and fast-paced story make this book an exciting read. I liked the character of Matt Deal because he reminded me of a young Charles Bronson."

Sources: <u>BookBub</u> and <u>Goodreads</u>

OTHER BOOKS BY STEPHEN BENTLEY

STANDALONE

Undercover: Operation Julie – The Inside Story

Death Among Us: An Anthology of Murder Mystery Short Stories

SERIES

The Steve Regan Undercover Cop Thrillers

*Who The F*ck Am I?*

Dilemma

Rivers of Blood

The Secret - COMING SOON

Detective Matt Deal Thrillers

Mercy

Mayhem - COMING SOON